meeTinGs wIth

thE arcHaNgEL

BY STEPHEN MITCHELL

Poetry
Parables and Portraits

Fiction
Meetings with the Archangel

Nonfiction
The Gospel According to Jesus

Translations and Adaptations
Real Power: Business Lessons from the Tao Te Ching *(with James A. Autry)*
Full Woman, Fleshly Apple, Hot Moon: Selected Poems of Pablo Neruda
Genesis: A New Translation of the Classic Biblical Stories
Ahead of All Parting: The Selected Poetry and Prose of Rainer Maria Rilke
A Book of Psalms
The Selected Poetry of Dan Pagis
Tao Te Ching
The Book of Job
The Selected Poetry of Yehuda Amichai *(with Chana Bloch)*
The Sonnets to Orpheus
The Lay of the Love and Death of Cornet Christoph Rilke
Letters to a Young Poet
The Notebooks of Malte Laurids Brigge
The Selected Poetry of Rainer Maria Rilke

Edited by Stephen Mitchell
The Essence of Wisdom: Words from the Masters to Illuminate the Spiritual Path
Bestiary: An Anthology of Poems about Animals
Song of Myself
Into the Garden: A Wedding Anthology *(with Robert Hass)*
The Enlightened Mind: An Anthology of Sacred Prose
The Enlightened Heart: An Anthology of Sacred Poetry
Dropping Ashes on the Buddha: The Teaching of Zen Master Seung Sahn

For Children
The Creation *(with paintings by Ori Sherman)*

Books on Tape
Meetings with the Archangel
Real Power
Bestiary
Genesis
Duino Elegies and The Sonnets to Orpheus
The Gospel According to Jesus
The Enlightened Mind
The Enlightened Heart
Letters to a Young Poet
Parables and Portraits
Tao Te Ching
The Book of Job
Selected Poems of Rainer Maria Rilke

meeTinGs wIth thE arcHaNgEL

a COmEdy oF tHe SpIRiT

StePheN miTChEll

 HarperCollins*Publishers*

HarperCollins books may be purchased for
educational, business, or sales promotional
use. For information please write: Special
Markets Department, HarperCollins
Publishers, Inc., 10 East 53rd Street, New
York, NY 10022.

FIRST EDITION

Designed and typeset by David Bullen Design

Library of Congress Cataloging-in-
Publication Data
Mitchell, Stephen, 1943–
Meetings with the archangel /
Stephen Mitchell.—1st ed.
p.   cm.
ISBN 0-06-018245-8
1. Gabriel (Archangel)—Fiction.
2. Zen Buddhism—Fiction.
3. Dialogues, American.
4. Angels—Fiction.   I. Title
PS3563.18235M44   1998
813'.54–dc21   98–18018

98   99   00   01   02   ❖/RRD
10   9   8   7   6   5   4   3   2   1

tO vіCkI

coNTentS

meeTinGs wIth thE arcHaNgEL

chAptEr I

hE WAS STANDING NEAR the little olive tree in front of my writing studio—wings, white robe, halo, everything, as if he had just stepped out of a Renaissance painting. The wings were huge: a dozen feet across. He fluttered them twice, then folded them carefully behind his back, like someone tucking a handkerchief into his breast pocket.

My first reaction was a shiver that began at the back of my neck and rippled down my spine. My second reaction was a silent "Oh shit!"

You may have heard of my book *Against Angels*, which stirred up a good deal of controversy a few years ago. (It was praised by all the wrong people, condemned by the Catholic Church, and, to my mild surprise, climbed up and down the New York *Times* bestseller list for ten weeks.) I'll tell you about it later, by way of explanation, and about myself as well, and how I arrived at being visited by the archangel Gabriel. For even before I saw the lily in his hand, I knew it was him.

I was disappointed, as you'll understand when you get to "The Six Angel Pictures"—disappointed not in myself, but in the level of my spiritual maturity. I had thought I was further along. To discover now, after twenty-two years of Zen training, that I was still susceptible to otherworldly visions . . . Ah, well. On the other hand, the event certainly had its fascination. And even in these first moments of our acquaintance, as he waited there politely, bathed in the sunlight of a northern California spring day, the upper edges of his wings overlapped by the silver-green leaves of the olive tree, I realized that there had been some excessive quality in my book, some attachment to a view of reality that excluded the muse of the archetypal, or at least banished her to an ash-strewn corner beside the kitchen fire.

"Fear not, Stephen," said the archangel, "for thy prayer hath been answered." He wore a robe of heavy, cream-colored satin. His face was girlish and white; it had the look not of human skin but of a flower petal; was, in fact, the same white as the lily in his hand, which seemed to be illumined from inside, as if there were a tiny light-source in its throat. Above his blond head floated a stiff circle of gold the size of a dinner plate.

I couldn't help raising an eyebrow. The Renaissance trappings, the King James language: it was all a bit

much. Besides, what prayer could he possibly be refer-
ring to?

As if he were aware of my thoughts, he tilted his head
and looked at me for a moment, quizzically, birdlike. I
heard a long, musical "Oh"—not an external sound, but
an "Oh" that resonated inside my mind like an arpeggio
played on a harpsichord. Then he was gone, and in his
place near the olive tree stood a seven-foot-tall ellipse of
light.

"Does this suit you any better?"

I didn't know what to say.

"In me," said the light, "as the miracle of understanding is effortlessly achieved, each single truth that I dis-
cern shines in the radiance of all truths, like jewels in the
crown of unitive knowledge. I am the intelligence that
ceaselessly consumes every created thing, without being
affected or changed by anything in return. Throughout the universe of my marvelously pure spiritual substance, all truths exist equally distant from one another
and from myself, in such perfection of their harmony
and correlations that even if I were to cease existing, the
system of their simultaneous necessity, glittering like a
diadem, would endure by itself, in all its sublime pleni-
tude."

This also, I realized, was a bit much: too condensed,
too exhausting, too (let's be frank) intelligent. And though
I had felt a certain pleasure in listening, it was the kind of
pleasure a dog might feel as his master spoke incompre-
hensibly endearing sounds to him.

Again an "Oh" like a harpsichord arpeggio; the ellipse

vanished; standing before me was a young man in his early thirties.

"Sorry," he said. "I usually get it right the first time." He looked at me sheepishly, with such a warm smile that I had to smile myself.

"Let's start over," he said, extending his right hand. "I'm Gabriel."

"Yes, I know," I said. "Pleased to meet you." His hand-shake was firm but fluid. I could feel a current of energy in his palm.

As I gazed at him, what struck me first was not his beauty but his nakedness. I work out four times a week at the gym and am quite used to being among naked men. But to be fully clothed and greet a naked visitor was something new. Briefly I considered taking off my own clothes so that he would feel more comfortable. But then it occurred to me that his present form was an effort to make *me* comfortable, and that the courteous response would be to do nothing.

He had chosen a beautiful, vaguely familiar body, about five foot ten, solid but graceful, with the long, firm muscles of a dancer. His face too was dazzlingly beautiful, masculine but not rugged—black hair, sensuous lips, high cheekbones, large finely-sculpted nose. It seemed Mediterranean and could have been an Israeli's, though the most compelling feature was the huge pale-blue animal eyes; I had seen eyes like that, not nearly so alive, on a friend's husky. I glanced at his penis. It was uncircumcised.

"May I offer you a chair?" I said. "Something to eat?"

"I'd love to sit down. And yes, I *am* rather hungry. I forgot what it's like to have a body."

I brought over two patio chairs from the deck, and a small glass-topped table, and returned in five minutes with a loaf of multigrain bread, fresh that morning from our town bakery, a half-eaten pasta salad my wife had made the day before, some baked tofu, a barbecued chicken breast, a bottle of a local Chardonnay and one of port, and a bowl of apples, bananas, and grapes. My ancestor Abraham, I remembered, had served an entire calf to his angelic visitors, but there was no word for cholesterol in ancient Hebrew.

"If there's anything else you want . . ."

"No," he said. "This is perfect."

I cut him a thick slice of bread and poured a glass of the Chardonnay. Then I sat down and watched him as he ate. He chewed very slowly.

When he had finished, he said, "Thanks, that was delicious. Eating is a kind of pleasure we don't have in heaven. This drama of need and satisfaction that repeats itself . . . how many times a day? What frail, marvelous creatures bodies are! Fearfully and wonderfully made."

How long was it since he'd last had a body? I thought this to myself, or maybe I said it aloud, because he answered, "A minute? A century? It's hard to keep track. My memory works for certain earthly events, but it doesn't have a sorting system. In heaven, there's no such thing as a *where* or a *when*. Entering space and time is, for us, like traveling to a very foreign country. All the rules are different."

I should remark that up to this point it took a considerable effort for me to keep up my end of the conversation. Actually, it was hard even to concentrate on what he was saying. I kept finding myself absorbed into the beauty of his face and into the extraordinarily enchanting musicality of his voice, rich and woody, as if a cello could talk. I would listen for a few moments, then get lost in it, then come back, then get lost again. Sometimes, to keep myself focused, I had to look off into my neighbor's field, with its grapevines and four cows grazing, or to the easy, oak-tufted hills in the distance. But eventually I was able to pay attention. Not that the dazzlement had grown any less, but my eyes and ears had gotten used to it, as in the minutes after you leave a movie matinee and step into the blaze of the midday sun.

"May I ask you another question?" I said.

"Please. Ask whatever you want."

"It's just that I'm wondering why you were sent. What message did you bring me?"

"No, no, it doesn't happen like that. We aren't sent; there are no messages. We simply appear in the mirror of someone's consciousness. Or, more accurately, we *are* the mirror. Later on, when they tell their story of the encounter, there is always a message that they find. Sometimes it's even more or less true."

"Then why did you come?"

"Don't you know?"

"I have a sense of it. But I want to know *your* reason."

"Let's say that I was drawn by a kind of spiritual gravity."

I paused to take this in, but couldn't quite grasp it.

"It's not complicated," he said. "Haven't you ever been in a crowd, and suddenly you feel you have to turn around to look, and you see someone already looking at you? It was like that: a magnetic pull that came to me in the midst of my games. Perhaps I was drawn by the brick path to your studio that winds between the olive and the apple tree. Or by the intensity of your marriage vows, or the way you hold your pen as you stare into the blank page of your notebook. Or by the unmingled flavor of your grief."

"So you didn't come to tell me anything in particular?"

"I have a lot to tell you. But I didn't come to tell you a thing."

"Hmm."

"I'd *like* to tell you about heaven. I'd like to *show* you."

"But why?"

"Read your book again after I leave. You'll see."

Against Angels, you should know, is not against angels per se. But it *does* take a stand against the sillier inanities of the current angel craze. I wrote it in a fit of exasperation at the sentimentality of the angel-watchers, good people though they might be, and my sense of spiritual priorities made me highly critical of the whole shebang. Of course, many reviewers attacked the book for undermining religion, for trying to destroy the innocent faith in the hearts of American children, and so on. One pious fellow called me "the Arch-Grinch." Another entitled his article NO, VIRGINIA.

I poured two glasses of the port and picked mine up. "I

9

hope you and the others didn't take my criticism person-ally."

"We enjoyed it, my dear. We came to bathe in your anger like birds in a puddle of rainwater."

"Well, I'm glad. I didn't mean to offend you. Though you're probably not offendable."

He picked up his glass of port, said "L'hayyim," and took a sip. "What's the title of your next book?"

"I guess it'll have to be *In Praise of Angels*."

"Oh, there's no need to apologize, you know. Nothing public. This visit is just for you."

"Or I could call it *The Unnecessary Angel*," I said, amused at the possibilities. "But tell me about heaven. What do you do? How do you spend the time—I mean the non-time?"

"What do you *think* we do?"

"I haven't got the foggiest idea. The way people talk about it, heaven is a long—a *very* long—Sunday service. And you angels are the church choir, singing hymns for ever and ever. And ever."

"Not a happy prospect."

"There's an anecdote—is it Bertrand Russell's?— about an Englishwoman who's asked where she thinks her dead husband is. 'Oh,' she sighs, 'I suppose he is en-joying eternal bliss. But let's not talk about such depress-ing things.'"

"Bliss," Gabriel said. "Do you know what it is?"

"Supreme joy. At least, that's what the *word* means. I've had my share of joy. But prolonged, unadulterated joy? Joy comes and goes. I keep my door unlocked."

"Well, I won't show you the feeling. Human bodies can't bear the intensity of it. But imagine the happiness of an ideal king, young and handsome, wise, rich beyond all desire, physically vibrant, honorable in every way, beloved by his people, adored by his many wives."

"Wait a minute." I closed my eyes and visualized the scene. Nice. Solomon in all his glory. The phrase reminded me of the lilies of the field. A field of lilies superimposed itself onto my mental screen. I made a small adjustment, and there was Solomon again, lounging on a waterbed in his harem. One gorgeous, bare-breasted wife was massaging his shoulders. Another was licking his left thigh. Another was defeating him at chess with a Nimzo-Indian defense. Another was explaining the fine points of a public health bill he was about to sign.

"Okay," I said.

"Now multiply that happiness by a million."

I tried. I couldn't even get to two. "You've lost me."

"If you could multiply it by a million again, and do that a million times, you'd have some idea of the bliss that even the least of the angels feel. And the greater our capacity, the greater our bliss."

"Not your everyday Sunday service."

"The essence of heaven is joy. Joy is the air we breathe, the ground of our meditation, the sky through which we soar. And the contemplation of God doesn't mean standing around staring at some deity. It's the most thrilling game you can imagine."

"Game?"

"For us, everything is a game," he said, "as everything

is the joyous contemplation of God, because whatever comes from God *is* God. So all our games are ways of contemplating different aspects of That Which Is. The simpler ones have to do with limits—creating and destroying them. Ultimately there are no limits except the ones we create for ourselves, and the limits of pure spirit, our angelic nature—which are, however, considerable."

"How so?"

"We're incapable of feeling sorrow, for one thing."

"Yes, that would be a bit of a limit," I said. "But one I wouldn't be too sorry to have."

"You might think twice about that. You don't yet understand."

"Understand what?"

"That I am here as your mirror."

This puzzled me. What did he mean? Where was my own image in that elegant body, wingless but graceful as air, in that face overflowing with delight like David's cup? I looked into his huge pale-blue eyes and could not see myself.

"But let me tell you about the games," Gabriel said. "In heaven, it's the easiest thing in the world to step beyond limits. Instantaneously I can expand my body . . ."

"Your body?"

"I beg your pardon, but I have to use the words of your very physical language. I can expand my energy field— what you might call my body—to include what in space would be the equivalent of the earth, sun, and solar system. Then I can expand further, to include the galaxy, then further until I include all space. And when I am that vast, I have only to look inside myself to see the ultimate curve of the universe or the primal birth of the stars."

"Yes, it *sounds* easy," I said.

"And that's only the physical aspect of the universe. I can do the same with the universe of thought, or with any of the other infinite modes in which reality manifests itself. But since that's hardly a challenge, after a while it's not much fun."

"After a while?"

"After a while, as it were. The challenge is in creating limits. It's like making rules for a sport. For example, I can will myself to *become* matter. For the tiniest flash of a moment, with a rush of excitement, I forget who I am. It's like a young child covering its eyes for a game of peekaboo, except that here I cover my primal identity. Suddenly I feel heavy, crushed. My flight slows, stops. I am falling, then wading, through a dense, gluey liquid. Then the wading stops. I acquire atoms and the space between atoms. I vibrate into time. The world grows heavier, nothing but mass and energy. I feel heavier and heavier, more and more crushed, bound by the laws of the physical, until I can't bear it any longer. And then, at the last possible instant, I remember who I am. And as soon as I remember, I burst into praise—flame or song."

"A star?"

"If you looked through a telescope."

"And I could hear you? If there were a telescope for the ear?"

"Give your ear enough room," he said, "and naturally you'd be able to hear me. And not only me. My song would have been picked up and repeated, with infinite variations, by infinite others playing the same game. We pass on the song from star to star, like whales."

"'When the morning stars sang together, and all the sons of God shouted for joy,'" I quoted. (*Job* was a book I knew intimately.)

"I would translate that not 'shout*ed*' but 'shout.' There is always a host of us exploding with joy at the first moment of creation, which has never ceased happening."

"Let me get this straight," I said. "This is the *simplest* kind of game?"

"Well, space-time, you know."

"What about the more complicated games?"

"I won't even try to describe what can happen in a game with another archangel, or with multiple players. It's glorious. Not ecstatic like our lovemaking—after all, if you step out of yourself, there's no game left—but truly glorious."

"What do you mean, 'our lovemaking'? Angels have sex? What *kind* of sex? How? What does it feel like?"

"Slow down, my dear. Not everything at once. Didn't you ask about games?"

"Okay," I said. "You're right. Please continue."

"Suppose you want to play with a truth. You can praise it, you can admire it, you can contemplate it from every possible viewpoint, you can vary it, you can taste it, you can ingest, embody, live it. And for all this while, that truth is the only reality in the universe. But then you take another truth and set it beside the first one. Because every truth has its opposite."

"Why not stay with the first truth?"

"Before there was One," he said, "there was Zero, and inside that circle dwells the mind of God. One is the creation of the world. But when you have a world, you have things. So once you have One, you have Two, and then, sooner or later, infinity, infinite infinities. These are not just concepts; this is what creation is all about. Before the beginning was the Zero; in the beginning was the One. And since Two is already implied, you get curious about what would happen if the One meets the Other. Besides, there are so many things you can play with. Everyone knows that opposites attract. Well, sometimes there's a kind of magnetic field between two opposite truths. You can use that to create something new. Or you can contemplate the two truths in such a way that they become one greater truth. They appear as if you were seeing the same thing with the right eye and the left eye, in a kind of depth vision."

"Hmm."

"But often there is no magnetic field, there's simply an abyss. One of our most exciting games is standing on the edge of a truth, just before it touches its opposite, and gazing down into the abyss between them. Each abyss has its own quality. It's not that there's nothing there, but that the gap is impenetrable even to an angel."

"That doesn't sound like much of a game."

"It's thrilling," he said. "You can't imagine what it's like for an infinitely pure intellect to come face to face with the unknown. Sometimes I will stand gazing down into the abyss for what to you would be centuries."

"Gazing at what?"

"It's not that kind of gaze."

"Ah. And then?"

"Then, slowly, I move to the edge of the abyss. I take one last, exhilarated, uncomprehending look down into it. I close what you would think of as my eyes. I spread what you would think of as my wings. And then I leap in head first, hurtling straight down into the deep space of oblivion, a black wind whistling past my ears in the motionless motion of my flight, my heart pounding, my voice crying out involuntarily with a shout in which victory and disaster are indistinguishable."

"Like skydiving?"

"If you can imagine skydiving into the equal-sign of an equation. Of course, for us there is no possibility of dying."

"Yes, well that *would* change things. Take some of the thrill out of it."

"Not at all. Death is highly overrated as a stimulant. Look at children: death is unreal to them, but they don't enjoy themselves any the less."

"True," I said. And then, as the thought occurred to me: "You angels seem as *active* as young children. Do all your games have to do with motion? Don't you ever sit still?"

"*Mostly* we do. But our stillness would still be beyond the range of your perception, since we vibrate much faster than the speed of light. And even our movement is not so much motion as *e*motion, thought-feelings flashing vividly through us as living truth. It doesn't happen in space, you see."

"I *don't* see. But that's all right. Tell me about the stillness. Is it a kind of meditation? 'Be still and know that I am God,' as the Psalmist says?"

"No, that's a verse for you restless humans. We are never *not* aware that the *I Am* is God, whatever we happen to be doing or not-doing. The still, small games are less exciting, but more exquisite. I can tell you about them, if you like."

"My head's spinning. Let me take a time-out first."

He nodded. I half-closed my eyes, focused my awareness in my belly, took a few deep breaths. Everything slowed down. The contents of my mind began to fade. I felt reconnected to the deep calm at the core of things. Five minutes or so passed.

I opened my eyes. For half a second there was no one facing me. Just an empty chair.

Then the archangel was there again. He had crossed his right leg over his left and was sipping from his glass of port. "Well done," he said. "Lovely."

"This has been a lot for me to take in."

"I know," he said, setting his glass down on the table. "Would you rather talk about something else?"

"Let me see." It *would* be a relief, I thought, if the conversation could shift, at least for a couple of minutes, to a lighter subject, one that wouldn't expand my sense of reality quite so fast. But how do you make small-talk with an archangel? Do you comment on the weather?

"Nice day, isn't it?" Gabriel said.

I burst out laughing.

"How do you think the Giants will do this year?" he continued.

"Okay, okay. No need to exaggerate."

"We could spend the time together in silence, if you'd prefer."

"No, I just needed to recharge my batteries. But speaking of weather, how *is* the weather in heaven?"

"It depends on the heaven."

"You mean there's more than one?"

"Yes," he said. "I've been talking about the heaven of the archangels. I didn't want to confuse you. There is also the heaven of the gods, the heaven of the animals, the heaven of the seraphim, the heaven of the interim— many heavens. I'll tell you about some of them another time. Not now. You'd get overloaded."

"Thanks. I appreciate it."

"But to answer your question. We do have weather in our heaven, if we want to create in a semi-physical world. Our weather is always perfect."

"Perfect how? Spring-perfect or summer-perfect? Are there fruits or are there blossoms on the trees?"

"Imagine your spring, summer, autumn, winter all together, all at once."

"I can't."

"You know how all colors come from white, through a prism, and return to white, on a spinning disk? It's like that: as if you put the four seasons on a disk and set it spinning."

"Ah," I said. But my mind refused to make the effort. "Tell me, what did you mean by 'if we want to create'?"

"Our principal games have to do with love and art. Art is, you might say, the creative contemplation of God."

"You don't mean that you sit there with semi-physical paintbrushes and semi-physical easels, do you?"

"No," he said, "it's all created and all enjoyed in the spirit. Some of your own artists do that: Mozart, for one, who can hear an entire symphony in his mind's ear before he ever sets down a note. But our art dances in and out of categories. For us, everything is connected to everything else. Even the most elementary angel might notice the affinity between birds and trees, say, or between an atom and a solar system, or between God as creator and God as created, and from that one perception a statue or a sutra is born. Or I can create something in the mediate realm between painting and molecular physics, for example, or between poetry and architecture. I once composed a string quartet out of a theorem of algebraic topology."

"What did it sound like?"

"I'd have to draw it for you. Besides, there's an essential aspect that I haven't touched on yet. The emotion that you humans feel for the beautiful, we feel for the good as well. We *see* the good as beautiful; for us there's no distinction. This is, after all, a moral universe. Do you feel like stretching?"

"I feel pretty stretched already."

"No, I mean your body. We've been sitting for quite a while."

We both stood up. I touched my toes a few times, then did a little t'ai-chi.

When I looked over, Gabriel was still stretching, arms and legs at forty-five-degree angles to the vertical and horizontal: the very image of Blake's *Glad Day*. I *knew* I'd seen that body somewhere before.

He sat down again. I did too.

"So," I said. "Tell me about angelic sex."

"Sex is one of the ways we contemplate God," he said, with a smile that glowed a kind of celestial rosy red. "It's our most intense game of mutual delight."

"Is it like human sex?"

"First of all, we don't have sex*es* as you do. There are no male or female angels."

"But..."

"Oh," he said, "this is the form I took for your sake. In our heaven we always start off with variations of the One, not the Two. So we're all one kind, though with infinite variations."

"In other words, you're homosexual?"

"Well, I suppose so, in the sense that *homo* means 'the same.' But it's more accurate to say 'metasexual.' We aren't looking for a partner to complete us. We're already complete. And in any case, our sexuality isn't genital. We don't have organs for that. We create, we don't procreate."

"How often do you have sex?"

"As often as we meet. We're not what you'd call monogamous."

"Ah. So it's true that the angels in heaven 'neither marry nor are given in marriage'? That's a Gospel saying I've never cared for. It would be a big problem for me. I must have a monogamy gene."

"No, it wouldn't be a problem, I assure you. You've learned to play faithfulness in one key, but there are thousands of keys to play it in. Anyway, the first thing you should understand is that we're all in love with the *I Am*. The reason our love is so pure is that we expect nothing in return. Love is who we are; we have no interest in *being* loved, though that is part of our joy. When you see God in all creatures, it's impossible *not* to fall in love with them."

"And what happens when you meet another archangel?"

"That's hard to describe in a physical language," he said. "It's not so much a falling in love as a rising in love, as if I were stepping from a three-dimensional to a five- or six- or ten-dimensional universe. When I first look into the beloved's face, I am reborn on the other side of myself. There's no longer an inner or an outer. Song bursts into song, color into color, the beloved becomes everything in the world, everything holy or unholy, the breath moving beside my breath, the heart beating in my heart. The whole universe has become a garden. Adam on a bed of moss, dreaming of night, moistness, the shadow of a rose. He wakes up to the pulse of his own fulfillment. All the leaves on the Tree of Life are tiny mirrors. In each mirror he sees Eve's face, O my dove, in the clefts of the rock, in the secret places of the stairs. The moon's blood flows in his veins. The whole garden is her body. Where can he find himself?"

"All this, before you come together?"

"This is the first moment, which lasts as long as we want it to."

"And when you do come together," I said, "there's nothing like genital union?"

"No. We unite with our whole bodies, easier than air

with air. There's no resistance. We surrender ourselves completely. We're lost in each other, found in each other. We taste each other's presence, hear each other's absence, whisper each other's most secret name into the heart of being."

"And your pleasure?"

"It's not concentrated in one place, as with you," he said. "We're suffused with it, penetrated by it, through and through; everywhere we brim over with each other's sexual joy."

"Do you have orgasms?"

"Any climax would be an anticlimax. No, our pleasure doesn't explode and dissipate; it goes on and on; galaxies are born and die during the circuit of our embrace. Our union is like one of your Bach melodies that moves with all its lines in long, sinuous counterpoint, each winding in and out of the others, each line, each note, complete in itself, until at the appointed time they all naturally come to an end in the final chord."

"Mmm."

"Of course, this lovemaking would be impossible with bodies of flesh. But I can show you something of what it's like. Do you want to try?"

This was embarrassing. How could I say No to an archangel? How could I say it politely? I felt a churning in the pit of my stomach.

Gabriel looked at me with a huge amusement in his eyes. Then, in less than a minute, his features softened, his hair grew long, his penis disappeared, breasts formed, his waist narrowed, his hips broadened, until he—she—

sat before my eyes with an hourglass figure rather like my wife's, though twenty years younger.

I felt much better. "Sorry," I said. It was hard not to stare.

"Please don't apologize," Gabriel said. Her voice was rich but higher now, like a viola. "It was my fault. I forgot how heterosexual you are."

"Yes, well . . ." It was a struggle to keep focused, with her stunning legs competing for my attention, her lovely full breasts. To add to the problem, there was an unequivocal stirring in my penis.

She burst into laughter. "Thanks, but let's make it simple." Immediately she was clothed in a lavender-colored cotton robe that covered her from shoulders to ankles.

"Would you like to try *now*? It doesn't even involve touching. Put your mind at ease."

I nodded.

"Let's find a comfortable place for you to lie on. How about over there, near the walnut tree?"

"That's fine," I said. "I'll be back in a minute."

I returned from the house with our old picnic blanket, spread it on the grass, and lay down.

Gabriel knelt on the blanket beside me, to my right. She held her hands out, palms downward, a foot or so above my heart. "Close your eyes," she said. And then, very gently, "Just let it happen."

As I lay there, I was aware of nothing out of the ordinary at first. The breath passed in and out of my nostrils with the tiniest of breezes, moved my belly up and down, grew slower and deeper as the minutes went by. All the drama of the encounter began to dissipate—the excitement, confusion, questions, answers—as my mind regained its composure. I was aware of Gabriel's presence behind my head, and I kept scanning for any sensation that might be the harbinger of something unusual. But after a while, I relaxed into the given. No thoughts, no feelings, the mind calm and open. My awareness sank deeper into my body. My breath breathed itself.

Then, almost imperceptibly, a kind of radiance appeared. It was faintly visible on my mental screen: like looking at the dawn sky, when the sun is just below the horizon and the edges of the world open toward the light. I could also feel it flowing through my body, from the feet upward, as if the blood in my capillaries were turning to liquid gold. It was an extremely subtle sensation at first, but the pleasure was intense, like what a woman must feel when her lover says *Don't move* and with his tongue slowly circles each of her breasts and circles each nipple and moves down across her belly and pubic hair and down her inner thigh and up again and lingeringly up her labia and clitoris and says *No, don't move* and slowly across her belly up to her nipples and begins again. Except that this was happening not just on the surface but throughout my body. As if from some source deep inside me, tiny waves of pleasure were rippling out to the edges of my awareness.

As I struggle to describe this to you, I grasp at language and come up with "like" and "as if." I'm not trying to be fancy. It's just that I can't find words to convey the quality of these vivid body-events. All I can do is point. It was like . . . It was as if . . .

I don't know how much time had passed when I realized that my breathing was deeper than I'd thought possible. Some kind of door in my throat or belly had opened. I would breathe very slowly in or out, but after a breath reached its stopping point there was a long time when no movement occurred, and I found myself hovering in the immensity of space. It was like being a child on a playground swing: each inhalation seemed to last for minutes, and swung me with a rush backward past the far recesses of my throat and through my head to the top of my skull; at the arc's peak the swing stopped, as if caught and held in the air by invisible hands; and then each exhalation swung me into the light, down my chest and loins and thighs and out the tips of my feet. It was like being a boat rocked on a warm ocean, except that the ocean was inside my cells. The feeling was more peaceful than I can express.

Gradually I also grew aware that I had somehow spilled out over my skin, and I could feel my body energy running through the space around me. I was literally occupying an area that extended for a foot or so beyond the limits of my physical body. I noticed this without surprise. It felt like the most natural thing in the world.

Since the first few minutes of the experience I hadn't been at all conscious of Gabriel, so absorbed was I in the intensity of these sensations. But now I felt her presence in the border of space that I had come to inhabit. It was as if one circle had penetrated the circumference of a second circle, and in the intersected area you couldn't tell which circle was which; or as if a glass of wine were pouring itself into a glass of water. Slowly her presence moved from that outer area into the rest of my body. As her energy flowed into mine, a kind of dance began, a minuet at an eighteenth-century ball, in which each partner, hands barely touching, moves in the same intricate pattern of steps. Sometimes the dance would turn into a game of hide-and-seek: she was there inside me, then gone, then there again. I would feel her as the moon or as a hawk diving into my eyes. Sometimes I would be overwhelmed by lust, would hear drums pounding, see huge wet vaginal lips. Then once again we would be partners gliding past each other in the subtlest of minuets. Throughout all the changes, I felt aroused all over to a profound, tingling aliveness down to the marrow of my bones. It seemed as if every cell had an erection.

But the pleasure wasn't just erotic. My heart was opening too, like a flower in sunlight. Often during these events I was on the brink of tears, deeply moved by this opening of the heart, even in the midst of all the erotic rapture. Everything was happening at once. I felt excited as I had never been before, but at the same time my heart kept opening out into the light, and I felt as if I were an infant gazing into its mother's radiant eyes.

The current of energy running through my body would at times feel too powerful, most acutely in my legs. It was as if a needle-thin hose had been attached to a spigot and the water turned on full blast. At times I felt like jumping out of my skin, or shouting *No more! No more!* It was almost unbearable.

At this point I could still distinguish what was me and what was Gabriel inside me. As to my own energy, there were different modes that would shift as my awareness shifted, the way light is both particle and wave. Not only was I adult and infant at the same time, I was male and female. That is, my sexual identity still felt male (*very male*—I seemed to have several million penises dispersed throughout my body); but the current was coming toward and into me, and I found myself mostly in the role of the yin, the receptive. Sometimes the direction changed, and suddenly I was the yang, the energy would rush out of me into her, and I would see the image of her face, or of my wife's face, cheeks glowing, eyelids flushed, eyes swimming in pre-orgasmic ecstasy. Or the current would begin to alternate back and forth, so that one instant I was male, the next female, the next male, hundreds of times a minute. During one very long period I was nothing but yin: the energy kept flowing one way, into me. At a certain point I grew uncomfortable. It wasn't that I didn't enjoy what I was being given, or that I couldn't accept so much erotic pleasure lavished on me. But I felt unbalanced, the way you might feel if a rich friend kept buying you extravagant gifts and you had trouble thinking of even the smallest favor you could do in return. Eventually I couldn't stand it any longer. The desire to give welled up in my throat like tears.

It took a considerable effort to move my lips. I could barely manage a faint whisper. "Would . . . you mind . . . if I put . . . my hand . . . on . . . your leg?"

"Not at all," she said.

But I couldn't move. My right hand just lay there. After a few moments, she took it and placed it on her calf. I was overwhelmed by the intensity of this lightest of touches. It felt as if I had taken her in my arms and was passionately covering her neck with kisses. This was the only time during the experience when I actually had an erection. I was embarrassed, then amused, to notice that my penis, in its blind innocent way, was lubricating. But I felt glad I had asked to touch her. It did balance the energy.

After this I could no longer tell the difference between her and me. There was just one immense wave of brightness, ebbing and flowing. I couldn't feel when my breath stopped or started, or even whether I was breathing. It didn't matter. My sense of body had now expanded to include miles of earth and sky, it seemed. I, we, were dancing through all that space, the space was dancing through us. Everything was alive and glowing with joy. The sky had a woman's face, unbelievably beautiful and loving. I kept opening my heart into it; the more I opened, the more deeply I was received, until there was nothing left to open, and I felt as if I had become the woman and were holding my smaller self, with infinite tenderness, in my arms.

I have no idea how long I spent in this state. By degrees the radiance subsided. I began to breathe normally again. I opened my eyes.

chAptEr **II**

THE FIRST TIME I EVER smoked broccoli
was with an ultra-Orthodox friend of mine who looked
as if he had stepped right out of *Fiddler on the Roof*. His
name was Saul Greenberger. I had met him through one
of my graduate school classmates, a woman in the Religious Studies Department who was writing a paper on
the psychology of conversion. Saul had grown up in an
assimilated middle-class Jewish family much like my
own, though his parents lived in Manhattan and mine in
San Francisco. After a spiritual crisis when he was nineteen, he had changed his name from Paul to Saul and
dropped out of Amherst to become the disciple of a
Hasidic holy man called the Berditchever Rebbe. He was
twenty-six and I three and a half years younger when we

first came to know each other. By then he had, to a considerable degree, been accepted by the Rebbe's community, although, according to Saul, they still considered him something of a goy. He certainly didn't look like one, with his chest-length reddish-brown beard and glossy sidelocks, his black caftan and the velvet yarmulke he wore at all times. His face—deep-brown eyes, punctilious lips, high cheekbones, long diplomatic nose, the nose a thoroughbred race horse would have if it were suddenly enchanted into human form—exuded character and had a distinctively Jewish soulfulness to it; it was a face so antiquely Jewish, scholarly with an ascetic tinge, that it often reminded me of a Byzantine icon. (When I once voiced the comparison to Saul, he wasn't thrilled.)

This took place in the spring of 1965, thirty years before Gabriel appeared. I don't want to dwell on the pleasures of smoking broccoli, a practice I discontinued, abruptly, in 1968. But I promised to tell you about my spiritual path, and broccoli was the beginning.

During the mid-sixties most of my friends, of course, were experimenting with such mind-altering or -restoring substances as mescaline, LSD, and peyote. I was rather square for my milieu and hadn't tried anything more psychedelic than sex, which I considered quite strong enough, thank you. Not that I had any moral judgments about drugs. But there was a longing in me for an experience of God, a longing that I had been aware of from the age of fourteen and that I couldn't imagine being satisfied by any drug-induced ecstasy. Maybe it was in the end an esthetic preference: finding God through the digestive tract, even if it were possible, seemed to me in bad taste, with a certain mechanical quality involuted into its essence, like writing a poem on a typewriter. There was also the question of legality. I cared about the law; Thomas Jefferson was one of my heroes; for a few weeks during my junior year at college I had airily, and with an embarrassing lack of self-knowledge, thought of going to law school, not in order to become a lawyer but to understand the Constitution with greater discernment. My friends had a more casual relationship to the law, and all this experimenting was fine for them, I thought. But for me to do something illegal for the sake of my own pleasure would have been wrong.

So my heart skipped a beat when I learned from Saul that broccoli could get you high, and that in fact the Berditchevers had been smoking it for two hundred years. There was an intricate week-long ritual that you had to observe in the preparation of the final, psychoactive substance. We would begin—he, his ample, fertile wife Esther, and I—by sitting in silence at the tan-and-brown-oilcloth-covered kitchen table on a Thursday night. (It had to be Thursday because it took me four and a half hours to drive from Cambridge to the Williamsburg section of Brooklyn, and with my Harvard schedule I could spare only one night plus the Sabbath; and it had to be after his four kids were asleep.) Each of us would be equipped with a large stalk of broccoli, a single-edged razor blade, a magnifying glass, and one of the pig-shaped wooden cutting boards that Saul had made, once upon a time, in his seventh-grade shop class and that he adamantly, guiltily, refused to throw out. Then we would close our eyes and Saul would start us on a song.

The Berditchever songs—*nigguns* they are called in Yiddish—are famous among the Hasidim for their strangeness and their power to move the heart. None of them has words. You sing them in a kind of Jewish scat, somewhere between humming and crooning, with good, open, bouncy syllables like "ya *da da da da da*" or "yum um *um um um um*." The tunes are lively, attractive in their own modest folkish way; but you can't begin to appreciate them until you've been singing one, over and over like a mantra, for twenty minutes or half an hour. When you start, the tune romps in your throat like a frisky dog. You can't help being amused by it, with a slightly condescending pleasure at first if you're a lover of Bach. But it's a jazz band, not the Philharmonic. It's the breath flaring out and out, not deepening into the rhythms of contemplation as with Gregorian chant. Before long the tune is hopping around in your chest, tickling your bronchioles, rapping its knuckles on your auricles and ventricles, paddling down the rivers of your blood on a rubber raft. You want to stay a little longer inside the garden of one note, you want to smell the flowers, nibble the grapes, but the tune won't let you, you're off to the next garden in a mad dash, then the next one and the next. Your lungs ferment, your heart swells like yeasted dough, the tune has cloned itself and sent bearded eye-patched scouts down to your belly, to your genitals, out to the tips of your fingers and toes, it has arrived at the north pole of your skull and planted a dozen jolly rogers in your brain, scarlet Stars of David with crossed bones underneath, which flap dizzily in the wind. By now you can barely stay seated. Every corpuscle in your body is leaping up and down. There's a revolution going on in your socks, or maybe it's an orgy. You feel like laughing, like crying, you want to move but you can't begin to figure out how, all you feel inside you is a vibration, the tune has hollowed out your body until there are no organs left, you're nothing but an echo chamber now, is it you singing the tune or the tune singing you? *Somebody* is singing, long after the singing has stopped.

A half hour, sometimes an hour, would go by like this. Then the momentum would diminish, come to a halt, and we would open our eyes.

The singing was an essential part of the ritual. Saul had tried preparing broccoli in silence. It didn't work. When he smoked the songless stuff, nothing happened.

The tricky thing about the process is that you have to slice off the tiny florets at the precise point where they blossom into dark-green buds, without leaving any of the spindly lighter-green stems on them. It's an incredibly delicate operation. If you leave even a hairsbreadth of a stem on, it's no good, you can ruin an entire batch. It takes some time to get the hang of it. At first you feel you need three hands: one for the broccoli stalk, one for the razor blade, one for the magnifying glass. But after a few weeks of practice, it starts to be a little easier. The real pros, the Berditchever men of over, say, forty, don't need magnifying glasses. Their speed is astonishing. They can get through five or six stalks in an evening.

Saul would say a blessing, and then we'd settle down

to business. I enjoyed the procedure, though I never became very proficient at it; usually, upon Saul's inspection, at least three-quarters of my florets would have to be tossed out. But it was a pleasure to concentrate so hard on such a small physical reality, while the ghost of the evening's tune still hovered in the silence. And there could be no interruptions. No getting up to stretch or pee or roll your neck or touch your toes. You had to continue with your stalk and the infinitesimal *pop!* of razor blade slicing through thinnest vegetable flesh until all the florets were completely off, even if it took you well past midnight, as it often did. But eventually, with the heap of little green buds in front of me, and Saul and Esther patiently waiting on either side of the kitchen table, I would feel the satisfaction of a difficult job, not well done, but done.

I never bothered to learn the details of the curing process. The florets, I know, had to be sun-dried for a specific number of hours, with the appropriate blessing said over them, then dried again, then mortar-ground, then again left in the sun for several hours with the appropriate blessing. This finally resulted in a coarse, greenish-brown powder slightly thicker than snuff. It was odorless in itself, but when smoked it had a faint, not unpleasant, taste of the steamed vegetable. We would take about a teaspoon's worth, sprinkle a couple of drops of wine onto it to make it cohere, then roll it up in cigarette paper. The jaunty blue joint-holding gypsy on the Zig-Zag cover looked like Saul.

We would get stoned late Friday afternoon, after showering and dressing in our finest clothes and just before we left for the Sabbath service at the Berditchever synagogue. We'd have to finish smoking before sundown, of course, since it's against Orthodox rules to have a fire on the Sabbath.

A broccoli high was always, for me, a very sweet feeling. Amid the green haze, I would find myself looking at the world from within my favorite verse from the Psalms, "O taste and see that the Lord is good." Reality itself seemed delicious. Colors were heightened, sounds and smells more intense, my theological questions were less intense, I could feel my longing ease a little, my heart begin to open, like someone sitting on the edge of his bed stretching, still groggy with sleep. The Hebrew prayers were no longer a series of naive complaints and petitions; I could slide into them as if into a hot tub and soak there up to my neck in devotion. Every syllable could bring tears to my eyes, because it was another way of saying "you." Every prayer was a love song to the hidden beloved.

The nine-block walk to the Berditchever compound passed in this kind of delighted devotional fog, as did the Sabbath service itself. We would get undressed in the bathhouse next door to the synagogue, lower our naked bodies into the tepid, funky water of the ritual bath, then dress again amid dozens of Hasidim putting on their knee breeches and white silk stockings, their fringed undervests and caftans and *shtreiml*s (the circular, fur-trimmed Sabbath hat) in a buzz of excited Yiddish. Inside the synagogue, as close-packed as a rush-hour subway car—each man draped in the private tent of his prayer shawl, sometimes with a son or grandson tucked inside like a baby kangaroo, all of them rattling through the prayerbook at breakneck speed, rocking back and forth or side to side in quick hiccuppy movements—we would wait for the grand entrance of the Rebbe. When he stepped into the room, the whole surging mass of bodies parted like the Red Sea.

Nevertheless, broccoli highs had their not-so-hidden cost. There was always an unnerving jolt when I came down from them, and a kind of dissonance. Yes, being stoned was a great pleasure. But what was the point? I felt no closer to God afterward than before. And even though the stoned world was more intense, more enjoyable than the normal one, it was certainly no clearer. In fact, it was more than a little fuzzy. A romantic haze descended over the mind. All you see is holy, all you need is love, yeah yeah yeah. "But in the morning, behold, it was Leah." The everyday world seemed less satisfactory then, and I was always left mildly disappointed. For example, one Friday evening, on our stroll to the Berditchever synagogue, Saul and I walked down a different side street than usual. Midway down the block, he poked me and, with a large grin, pointed to a store across the street. The sign above it read, in gold letters on a black background, *Universal Reality Company*. "Wow!" I said, "I never knew there was a *store* for it!" But, of course, when we went back the next day to see what products they were offering in the marvelous store, the sign read *Universal Realty Company*. It was like that.

Still, the Friday-night dinners were a delight. Esther

would serve the usual Orthodox disaster of overcooked chicken and vegetables with the life boiled out of them (broccoli not often among them), but it always tasted good, as did the thick, over-sweet kosher wine, which in my normal consciousness I would have considered an absurd parody of port. There would always be a great deal of energetic singing, and conversations that scurried in and out of mystical theology, especially Benjamin ibn Ezra's *The Inner Garden*, which Saul considered the text of texts. On these occasions I got to know a few of the older members of the community, widows and widowers who had a standing invitation to come. One elderly man, a retired diamond merchant who had met me only once before, took me aside after dinner one evening and, out of the blue, volunteered to pay tuition and expenses for my remaining three years of graduate school, saying that it would be an honor to support such a bright, pious young man. I can't remember how I wriggled out of his offer without revealing how very un-pious, in Orthodox terms, I was. But I felt touched by his generosity.

The most regular Sabbath guest was a widower named Zusya Cohen, who became my guide to Jewish mysticism. How he managed to live in both the world of the Berditchevers and the secular world—he taught in the Department of Near Eastern Languages at Brooklyn College—I could never figure out, and I had to marvel that a passionate follower of the Rebbe could be so open-minded about Buddhism, Taoism, Islam, and even to some extent about Christianity. He was well into his sixties, a short, plump man, maybe five foot three, with a long silver-white beard and long silvery sidelocks that corkscrewed down his cheeks (for worldly affairs he would fasten them under his yarmulke with a bobby-pin). His hooked nose, large ears, and thick lips gave him a perfect anti-Semitic caricature of a face, but so animated, lit up with such sweetness and good humor most of the time, that it seemed to me almost beautiful.

Three years after I met him, at the end of a long, boisterous Sabbath discussion about God and evil, in which I had made a nuisance of myself by pointing to the Holocaust amid all the rapturous, broccoli-flavored praise, Zusya invited me out for a walk. It was autumn. I had recently gotten my Ph.D. in comparative literature—my dissertation was a study of the devil in *Paradise Lost*, the poetry of William Blake, and Goethe's *Faust*—and I was on my way to Berkeley to begin my teaching career. We strolled along the disheveled streets of Williamsburg, he in a black silk caftan and *shtreiml*, both of us with our hands clasped behind our backs. It had been a good six hours since we'd smoked. The only high I felt was from the gaiety of the Sabbath itself, the food and wine and singing and good fellowship.

"I don't usually mention this," Zusya said, "but you're a sincere young man, and I can sense your longing. What if someone offered you an experience of God?"

There was a rush of tears in my throat. "I've been waiting for such a long time," I said.

"Would you accept, even if it made your problem worse?"

"What do you mean?"

"An experience of God may be ecstatic. But it may just as well be devastating. We can never tell."

Now I was really bewildered. "What are you talking about, Reb Zusya?"

And he told me about a certain variety of wheat, grown in the hills around the holy city of Tsfat (Safed) in Galilee, blessed with kabbalistic prayers when it was sown, when it was reaped, when it was ground into flour, and when, in Brooklyn, every few years, it was baked into a single loaf of the braided Sabbath bread called hallah. "This hallah is very strong," he said. "I have taken it myself only five times and almost never offer it to students. But I think you may be ready."

I felt my face flushing. "Thank you, Reb Zusya. I know I am." I could barely contain my excitement.

"Don't thank me yet," he said. "You'll have to pay a price. There is always a price."

"What kind of price?"

"You can't see God's face without dying. Are you ready to die?"

"Yes," I said blithely, without the faintest notion of what I was getting into. I remembered what Blake had once written alongside a lovely, wingless angel he had drawn beneath his signature in an autograph album: "William Blake, one who is very much delighted with being in good Company. Born 8 Novr 1757 & has died several times since." But in my great ignorance, I didn't ask anything more.

We agreed that I would come back in a month, just before Yom Kippur.

I spent the time in Berkeley preparing for my adventure, fasting, praying, reading Blake and Isaiah. Only once did I hear from Zusya, a postcard:

Remember that God has a dark face too. The Abyss is another name for the Garden.

Study this story from the Talmud (Hagigah 14b): "Four entered Paradise: ben Azzai, ben Zoma, Akher, and Rabbi Akiba. Ben Azzai gazed and died. Ben Zoma gazed and went mad. Akher gazed and became an apostate. Only Rabbi Akiba entered in peace and departed in peace."

Rabbi Akiba departed in peace because he knew that even the absence of God is God. Love, Zusya

I flew to New York two days before Yom Kippur. I was overbrimming with excitement, and when I saw Zusya I couldn't help throwing my arms around him. "Yes, yes," he said, gently disengaging himself. "Welcome. But there's something we have to do before we can proceed."

"Oh?"

"Come." And he led me to a table at the back of his living room. On it was a small rectangular object wrapped in a red-and-yellow tulip-patterned silk kerchief. He untied it and took out a book and three old Chinese coins.

"The I Ching," he said. "I always consult it before something big."

I knew of the I Ching, had read Jung's foreword, had even learned the coin method of divination from a friend in my department who took the text seriously. After trying it a couple of times, I decided that it was sophisticated mumbo jumbo.

"Here," he said, handing me the three coins. And he told me to concentrate, clear my mind, then throw them. I did this six times, and after each cast he wrote down a number. Then he drew a hexagram, opened the book, and read. I could see his face drop. "It's no good," he said with a sigh.

"What?!"

"Listen," he said. "You threw number 6, *Conflict*. Here is the hexagram." And he pointed to it:

"The text says, 'You are sincere and are being obstructed. A cautious halt halfway brings good fortune. Going through to the end brings misfortune. It furthers one to see the great man. It does not further one to cross the great water.' I suppose I should try to get you an audience with the Rebbe. But it would be foolish to proceed with the hallah right now."

"Are you serious?" I said. "I don't mean to be disrespectful, Reb Zusya, but this is bullshit. It's totally arbitrary. Anyway, we had an agreement. I flew here all the way from California!"

"I'm really sorry. But I have been questioning the I Ching for twenty years now, and I've learned to respect its judgment."

"God*damn*it! Of all the ignorant, superstitious nonsense..."

"Look," Zusya said. "I know how disappointed you

are. But there must be a good reason for this. Why don't you take a walk and cool off? We'll talk later."

It was obvious that I wasn't going to argue him out of his decision. I walked for two hours, seething. When I got back, the living room was empty.

I went over to the table at the back of the room, opened the I Ching, read the judgment again, and slammed the book shut. Then I glanced at Zusya's worksheet. 8 7 8 8 7 7, broken straight broken straight straight straight. Wait a minute: the fourth line: he'd gotten it wrong! I had thrown a different hexagram! My breath almost stopped as I looked it up on the chart, then turned to the text. 59, *Dispersion*.

$$
\begin{array}{c}
\rule{2em}{0.08em}\ \rule{2em}{0.08em} \\[2pt]
\rule{0.85em}{0.08em}\ \ \rule{0.85em}{0.08em} \\[2pt]
\rule{2em}{0.08em}\ \rule{2em}{0.08em} \\[2pt]
\rule{0.85em}{0.08em}\ \ \rule{0.85em}{0.08em} \\[2pt]
\rule{0.85em}{0.08em}\ \ \rule{0.85em}{0.08em}
\end{array}
$$

"Success. The king approaches his temple. It furthers one to cross the great water. Perseverance furthers." Yes!! I ran out of the room, whooping.

The next day was the eve of Yom Kippur. After a fine dinner at his daughter's house (fine not because of the food, naturally, but because of the company and the Berditchever songs that kept bursting out in the midst of the talk), Zusya took me to his basement study. It was a musty, windowless room with a desk in one corner and two very old brown leather armchairs in the middle. Standing on an altar to the left of the desk was a miniature Torah scroll covered in gold-stitched purple velvet. Books lined the back wall from ceiling to floor; the other walls were filled with dozens of framed Hebrew inscriptions. A kabbalistically-engraved silver hand, with six silver handlets, dangled from the ceiling like a windbell.

Zusya walked to the altar and, picking up the half-slice of stale hallah that lay there, called me over to him. For a few minutes we stood side by side, hands clasped around the hallah, eyes closed. Then, after reciting the blessing for eating bread and the blessing for new experiences—to the God *shehekheyánu v'kiymánu v'higiyánu laz'mán hazéh*, "who has granted us life and sustained us and allowed us to arrive at this moment"—with an exhilaration and fear that made my heart pound, I bit into the hallah. By the time I finished eating it, chewing each mouthful slowly and with all the deliberation I could muster, Zusya had recited a few additional prayers, including the blessing for departing on a journey, and told me that, although he would be with me all night, available in case I needed help, from now on I was essentially on my own. And he went over to the bookcase, picked out a volume, and sat down in one of the armchairs, with a crackle of old leather.

Since I didn't feel anything special, I busied myself with inspecting the inscriptions on the walls. One of them in particular caught my attention, and I found myself staring at it for what seemed like a very long time. Some early Renaissance master of Hebrew calligraphy had written out the complete text of the Song of Songs on a small parchment page, about a foot and a half high by a foot wide. But rather than in conventional right-to-left horizontal lines, the verses were fashioned into interlocking geometrical shapes. Standing alone in the center of the page, surrounded by a frame of lines that became typographical braces to the left and right, was the word *shir*, "Song," the upper tips of each letter blossoming into a three-flowered bouquet. The rest of verses 1 and 2 ("of Songs, which is Solomon's. Let him kiss me with the kisses of his mouth: for thy love is better than wine") was inscribed around the first word, a circle about four inches in diameter, inside which two opposite-pointed triangles —verses 3 to 6, written in much smaller script—formed a Star of David. Around the first circle were six half-circles of verses, each of them beginning and ending at the point of a triangle. This central shape—"Song," Star of David, circle, half-circles—was surrounded by a large circle of larger letters, which in turn was surrounded by another large circle of tiny letters, which was itself surrounded by forty-three half-circles (I counted them twice), until I felt I was looking at the wrinkled yellow page through the peephole of a kaleidoscope. In addition, there were three large rectangles of verses, tiny/large/small, framing the whole design along the outer edges of the page, and in each of the four corners of the inner rectangle was a three-layered quarter-circle of verses, tiny/large/tiny. Inside each quarter-circle, drawn in lines rather than Hebrew verses, and perched on a flowering branch, a bewildered-looking dove gazed toward the center of the page as if for elucidation.

Had an hour passed as I stood there looking? Three hours? I'd lost all sense of time and suddenly realized I was feeling a bit woozy. So I walked over—along an invisible tightrope, it seemed—to an armchair, and very carefully lowered myself down. In the chair across from me Zusya was asleep. A large iridescent Hebrew book lay face-down across his thighs.

By now my whole body was vibrating from the inside, although when I looked at it from above, it appeared to be perfectly still. From above? Well, "above" is not the right word, nor is "outside." I was seeing myself from several directions at once, as if one "I" were a spectator from a spacial dimension at a slight angle to our normal three, and the other "I" were a Cubist painting. It was disorienting but quite funny. I heard a low gurgle of laughter slither across the floor.

I tried to pray, but my mind wouldn't stay put. The word "God" seemed weird. The word "I" seemed weirder. I looked around at the walls. They were rubbery. I could see them breathing in and out. The inscriptions wouldn't stay put either. Two of them were spinning like phonograph records. From the center of the silver hand an eye stared back at me. All of this seemed fascinating and supersaturated with meaning. But when I reached out for the meaning, it vanished.

Then my eyes fastened on the figure of Zusya slumped in his armchair, lightly snoring, a black velvet yarmulke on his head, sidelocks curling down past his shoulders, hands clasped across his belly, the large book pitched like a tent across his thighs. He too was looking very strange. Was he dead? Was *I* dead? The room felt cold enough to be a meat locker. Who was he anyway? I knew I loved him, but my love seemed to be clumped up somewhere in a corner of the room. As I looked deeper into his face, it started to change. Maybe it was my eyes that were changing. But it wasn't his face anymore. I saw another one behind it, and then another, and another. It felt as if I were on a down escalator looking across into the faces on the stairs going up. The speed kept increasing: *click* a Nordic face, *click* an African, *click* an Asian woman's, two men, three women, an infant's. Were these faces previous incarnations? Faster and faster they appeared, a different face rushed by every second, tens, hundreds of faces per second, *clickclickclickclickclickclickclick*, a wheel of faces rolling through his face faster than my eyes could grasp. And then, all at once, like a slot machine whirring to a halt, they stopped. There was only one face. It was Zusya's.

But how painfully, how piercingly ugly the face was. That hooked nose, those gross blubbery lips: a real kike's face. As I stared at him, I felt more and more nauseated, as if his repulsiveness were entering my organs like rotten food. There was a nausea of the heart as well. It was like looking at a rat in human form. He was oozing with malice, hatred, lewdness, every kind of moral filth. Putrefying flesh, the unbelievable putrid rottenness of him. I could feel a righteous hatred welling up inside me. He and his kind were cunning, treacherous, without a shred of human decency, and were bent on corrupting everything noble and pure in our culture. They had always been evil. Now they were plotting to rule the world. They had to be exterminated before they could spread their Jew filth and corruption any further. I was the hero who could destroy them before they destroyed us. And from the soil I could see my determination rise like a tree of thought, branching out into ideas, the ideas branching out into images, yellow stars, riots, broken glass, beatings, blood, cattle cars, naked rat-women and rat-children huddled on line, the disinfecting gas, the purifying smoke. And surrounding it all, in a glow of deep pride, my own honor at cleansing civilization of the deadly plague.

Then, abruptly, I was myself again: frozen with horror.

But horror is too mild a word. It is impossible to describe how appalled I was. Even though that glimpse through Hitler's eyes had lasted for only a few moments of clock-time, it seemed endless, indelible.

The rest of the night was agony. I know now that if my mind had been open enough, the obscene vision would have moved through it without harm, without residue, like any other mind-event. But at that time, I understood nothing. I couldn't bear what I had seen. I felt mortally ashamed. And because I stiffened into terror and self-judgment, the energy of the experience was cut off at the source. My mind cracked. I had been so deeply frightened that I didn't know where I was. I thought I had gone insane like ben Zoma in the Talmud and that I would never come back. I also remember being stuck in a Humean nightmare, convinced that—since the laws of causality are mere probabilities—just because the sun had always risen in the past, there was no assurance that it would rise this next morning, that in fact it was not going to rise, ever again, and that the earth had been plunged into its final darkness. Five or six hours passed this way. When dawn came, I burst into tears of relief.

Zusya woke up an hour or so later. He took one look at me and said, "Oy, *reboyneh shel oylum*, what happened? What happened, *neshumeleh*?"

I couldn't tell him. I could barely talk at all. I spent the whole day in a state of horrified numbness. Yom Kippur came as another kind of relief. All the melodrama of contrition and atonement made me smile wryly to myself, so pathetic did it seem. I felt absolutely alone.

I could see that Zusya was getting more and more concerned. Finally, he arranged for an emergency audience with the Rebbe.

I told the Rebbe what had happened. He listened with downcast eyes, nodding and swaying slightly. I knew that he had suffered greatly during the Holocaust, that he had lost his wife, four of his six children, and three-quarters of his community, to the ovens. He spoke very softly. He advised me to pray in the prescribed manner three times a day, to keep the commandments strictly, to do charitable work, and to ask God's forgiveness. But there was a moment, just after I had finished my account, when he looked up at me with undisguisable contempt. The look hit me in the face like a gob of spit.

2

I am telling you these stories to help you understand what strengths and absences in me might have elicited a

visit from an archangel. But stories are like the mountains in a Chinese painting: a few lines surrounded by the
immensity of empty space. That is true of even the most
dramatic human lives, so vast and subtle is the hidden
self, so deep are the roots of event. What is most important happens outside the stories.

I went back to Berkeley still aghast. Over the next
months, thanks to my teaching routine and perhaps also
to some volunteer work that I did at a soup kitchen, following the Rebbe's suggestion, my mind stitched itself
back together into some semblance of order. But I sorely
needed to understand what had happened. Was the vision no more than a demonic mockery of everything I
held sacred as a Jew? Or was it somehow what Zusya
had warned me about: a glimpse of the dark face of God?
And if so, how had I failed? What would it mean to walk
into the mind of Hitler and return in peace, like Rabbi
Akiba? All I knew was that I had been broken. I couldn't
fathom how the Abyss might be another name for the
Garden.

At this point, since I had no person who could help me,
I went to the Western classics for help, the only classics I
knew. My reading had been wide enough so that without
too much searching I could put my finger on two passages that spoke to my situation. There was a line from
the Latin playwright Terence: "Since I am human, I consider nothing human alien to me." And Goethe's brave
admission: "I have never heard of any crime that I myself
might not have committed." These became verbal talismans for me. They didn't help relieve my shame or hor-

ror, but they seemed to point me in a direction, although I couldn't tell what the next step in that direction might be. The only certainty I had was that my naive incomprehension of evil had been violently snatched away. I now knew only too well how such things could happen.

I spent the next five years in a considerable amount of psychic pain, aching for an insight into my experience. The problem of evil, which, before, had been harsh but manageable, now felt like a crushing weight on my mind. I thought that if I couldn't understand it, I would die.

I don't want to make this difficult period out to be gloomier than it was. I wasn't depressed in a clinical sense, or incapacitated in any way. I taught my Berkeley courses (pretty well, I think), hung out with writer friends at the cafés on Telegraph and Shattuck Avenues, read the morning paper, laughed, cried, took an active part in the anti-war movement, played squash twice a week, did volunteer work, went to academic parties and not-so-academic parties. I even finished my first book, *1672*, which was published in 1972 and had a modest but gratifying succès d'estime. It was a study of Spinoza, Vermeer, and Yaakov Vitale, one of my wife's rabbinic ancestors, who lived in Amsterdam, posed for Rembrandt's beautiful, Jewish Jesus in 1660, and later wrote a treatise on God as divine nothingness. The action takes place on a single summer day in Amsterdam, The Hague, and Delft. I described each man at the age of forty (all three were born in 1632) and interwove my study of their work with stories about my own three-month visit to the Netherlands and about Elizabeth's family, so that the book is an odd combination of travel journal, philosophico-theological exegesis, art criticism, and para-autobiography. I especially enjoyed imagining them as they went about their everyday business, as they created and occupied their very different worlds in the same segment of space-time, unaware of one another's existence, yet so complementary that it's breathtaking: Spinoza the right eye of wisdom, rational, unitive, dazzlingly clear, with a prototypical Jewish passion for justice and so profound an insight into God that for a century and a half he was branded a dangerous atheist; Vermeer the left eye of wisdom, with his Apollonian yellows and blues, the lyricism of his serenity (B minor to Spinoza's C), his variations on the single theme of a woman standing free in her own space, so meticulously observed and yet so inner that I used to call them collectively *Portrait of the Soul: At Home*; and Vitale the third eye, ardent, windowless, multifaceted as a fly's, and, as I much later realized, only halfway open.

A good deal of pleasure and some fulfillment accompanied the intense pain of those five years. But it was as if all the events—the teaching and writing, the friendships and grocery-shopping, the lovemaking, the marriage— were happening at one level of consciousness, and at another level I was deeply unhappy, unremittingly distraught and baffled about the evil in the world, which was also, somehow, in me. At that time I don't think I ever saw a photo of Hitler without shuddering. Or a photo of Holocaust victims without feeling my heart seized and wrung dry. The most difficult aspect of this

pain was that in addition to my doubts about God's goodness—or, at times, His sanity—it was impossible for me
to stand in a position of moral outrage. I could still *feel*
the outrage, but it wasn't a solid place, because the crime
wasn't something that "they" had done to "us." I had
done it too, in some sense, or I easily could have, had I
been brought up in different circumstances. This realization was beyond my ability to reconcile with my everyday emotions. I could still be generous to my students,
protest the war with fervor, consider myself a good
American and a faithful Jew, but there was an essential
disjuncture in my mind. The only time I felt even partly
whole was while making love.

I returned to the issue again and again, couldn't help
returning to it, like a tongue to a missing tooth. I read
constantly, searching for an answer. I thought that somewhere an answer must exist, somehow it had to be possible to know the truth so as to include all of human
experience in a vast embrace. I studied the Bible from beginning to end, I studied whatever mystical texts I could
get my hands on, and the principal classic and modern
Jewish theologians. None of them seemed even remotely
adequate. No one had *seen*, no one knew the answer in
his bones. The only text that spoke to me was the Book of
Job.

From 1969 through the spring of 1973, I read *Job* at
least four times a year. It was slow going at first, since the
Hebrew is always difficult and often textually corrupt,
and I had to spend a lot of time slogging around in my
Koehler-Baumgartner Lexikon. But the book had a mag-

netic fascination for me. Most of us, I think, are moved by the figure of a good man who suffers for no good reason, who is pushed to the brink of madness by the destruction of his possessions, his children, and his health. There was something extra for me, though. Because Job is the archetypal victim, his story seemed truly prophetic: it was the perfect parable of the Holocaust. I saw him as the embodiment of European Jewry, although, in the extreme compression of the ancient Hebrew verse, he couldn't help but be a more savage and eloquent figure than the real people who survived or died in the gas chambers. In expressing every emotion that the wreckage of a good life could elicit, from outrage to grief to disappointed love for God, he was for me a more appropriate representative of the victims than Anne Frank, with her innocent, pre-concentration-camp faith in humankind, (as dearly as I loved her) could be. His accusation struck me as the simple truth: "God doesn't care about us; he murders both the guilty and the blameless." Many years later, looking back at the figure of Job, I realized that he was giving voice to my own sense of confusion and anger at God, that the essence of his speeches is a heartbroken Fuck-you, expressed with such purity that it becomes a sacred gesture, as if someone were to carve a statue of the Buddha on which, instead of a smile, there is an agonized grimace, and instead of the mudra of palms-flat/thumbs-touching, one fist is held up toward God with the middle finger upraised.

But that wasn't the aspect of *Job* that riveted my attention. What thrilled and perplexed me was that this poet had *seen*. I knew it without a doubt. I could sense it, like a carnivore sniffing game in the wind. It was there, in the magnificent finale of the book, the Voice from the Whirlwind: not *a* particular insight into evil, but *the* insight, the essential one, the one I so desperately needed. It wasn't in the words themselves; it was underneath the words. The words issued from that knowing, like plants from the dark soil. Reading the Voice from the Whirlwind, over and over, from year to year, I felt as if there were something on the tip of my tongue, something deeply familiar that I couldn't gain access to. Or as if it were music playing in a distant room, so softly that I could barely hear it even when I strained, yet so distinctly that I knew it would make my heart sing if only I could get near enough. The insight had to do with a God that was far more vast than what I had been able to conceive of. This God was beyond good and evil, yet felt a fierce delight in Its creation, and in some fit of divine exuberance had created Leviathan and Behemoth, the two great embodiments of evil. It could catch Behemoth on a fishhook like a sardine and played fetch with Leviathan as if evil were the aquatic equivalent of a pet dog. "I form light and create darkness," as the *Job*-poet's colleague Isaiah has God say, "I make peace and create evil: I am the Lord." In other words, "I create mass-murderers and Crusaders and fanatics and Stalin and Hitler and other genocidal maniacs, and I play with them like toys: I am the Lord."

That there was a genuine answer in the Voice from the Whirlwind I was certain. But what the answer was, I didn't have the faintest idea. It was a complete mystery.

I returned to it again and again, but I could not penetrate. Inhabiting *Job* for these four years was like opening my eyes for the first time, only to discover that I was in total darkness.

Yet as hindered as I felt in some essential part of myself, the rest of my life moved ahead with unruffled momentum. I had met Elizabeth de Leon in Cambridge in 1967. We were married three years later. I told a version of our story in *1672*, and there is no need to retell it here. But I do want to mention one aspect.

When I fell in love with Elizabeth, it was more for her inner than for her outer beauty, appreciable as that was, especially the beauty of her lustrous Song-of-Songs eyes. But she had an additional luster for me even before I was introduced to her. I'd heard about her and her three sisters through the Harvard-Jewish grapevine, and about their family, which had been prominent in Jewish Spain and Italy for seven hundred years, not for its money or power but for its learning. I had met a few English and European aristocrats in Cambridge and abroad—charming, materialistic, arrogant people—and wasn't easily impressed by lineage; yet I was deeply moved by hers. Her father's family traced its origins to an eleventh-century rabbi in the kingdom of Granada and then to Moshe de Leon (the thirteenth-century author of the most important text in the history of Jewish mysticism, the *Zohar*), whose descendants had emigrated to Italy after the expulsion of the Jews from Spain in 1492. On her mother's side she came from a line of rabbis that began in ancient Rome and wound its way through the hill towns of Umbria and Tuscany, to Hayim of Verona (1502–1556), one of the inner circle of the kabbalist Isaac Luria and author of *Etz Hayim* (which means both *The Tree of Life* and *Hayim's Tree*), a long commentary on Genesis 2 and 3, one of those theosophic texts in which a few brilliant insights are buried in heaps of complicated thinking, like diamonds in a dunghill, as Jefferson said of the Gospels. Her father had survived the War with great hardship, and only because a peasant family near Turin had hidden him for two years in the loft of their barn. Her mother's people, by contrast, had emigrated to America in the early eighteenth century and established themselves in Massachusetts and Rhode Island as doctors, lawyers, and merchants. The most distinguished of them was Abraham Segrè of Newport (1751–1813), who fought in the Revolution, became an architect—his neo-Palladian synagogue is still in use—and wrote a famous letter to Jefferson on freedom of religion.

My fascination with Elizabeth's ancestors was, in one sense, a delving into the genetic past of the woman I loved, and it gave me the kind of poignant, slightly disoriented pleasure that I got from looking at photos of her as a little girl, in the old house on Fayerweather Street, with her sisters and cats and books and dolls and the always mischievous intelligence of her gaze. Elizabeth herself couldn't have cared less about her illustrious forebears. She was amused at *my* interest, and used to call me a snob-in-law. The only person from her family's past whom she found intriguing was her paternal great-grandmother's younger cousin, Modigliani the painter.

(Modigliani also gave her an instant rapport with my mother, who at first could hardly believe that "Italian" didn't necessarily mean "Gentile." I introduced them to each other in May of 1968, when my mother flew to New York for her great success, a show of her animal sculptures in the windows of Tiffany's on Fifth Avenue. We spent several hours a day in front of the windows, talking about Modigliani and Brancusi and Henry Moore, listening to the comments of the crowd as the animals stood in their unaccustomed splendor, the granite ostrich blushing under its canopy of diamonds and pearls, the green marble polar bear staring like Narcissus into an emerald pool.)

But my fascination was also a way of creating for myself a more intimate connection with the Jewish past, since my own family history petered out beyond my great-grandfather's generation in Odessa. I sometimes thought that Elizabeth had been given to me as a way into the deep places of Judaism, that through her, by a process of carnal osmosis, I would somehow, magically, have access to the wisdom of her ancestors. I suppose I hoped that in marrying her I had married them. It didn't work that way, of course. My answer wasn't hiding anywhere in the multitudinous and bastardized Aramaic of the *Zohar* or in the elegant Renaissance Hebrew of *Etz Hayim*.

But after three years of marriage, I felt an inner permission to look elsewhere for my answer, since I couldn't find it within the Jewish tradition. Before that, I would have felt disloyal if I had stepped beyond its boundaries.

True, I had been immersed in Western high culture for fifteen years; I knew Homer, Dante, and Shakespeare incomparably better than I knew the Talmud, which seemed to me about as spiritual as the telephone book; I admired Washington and Jefferson far more than Moses or Elijah; my interior landscape was peopled *mostly* by Gentiles, the airwaves were filled with Bach and Mozart, the walls with Vermeer and Matisse. But when it came to religion, I wouldn't have touched Christianity or Buddhism with a ten-foot pole. To find an answer is in a sense to become the answer, and I had been afraid of becoming something other than a Jew. Now, as the husband of the great-great-etc.-etc.-granddaughter of Moshe de Leon, I felt I could allow myself to explore outside.

This decision came gradually, after the honeymoon glow had worn off our marriage and we had been plunged into the difficult work and deeper joys of intimacy. Spinoza's God was my transition: to the God beyond God, to panentheism and meta-theism and non-theism, the unimaginably profound, subtle, luminous world of what mainstream culture still calls "Eastern" spirituality. I had discovered Spinoza in 1970. I can still feel the electricity of that first encounter.

I was standing by the bookcase in my old apartment in Berkeley, holding a copy of a paperback edition of the *Ethics* that I had bought that afternoon, for fifty cents, in one of the used-book stores on Telegraph Avenue. I had opened the book to a proposition in Part 1, then flipped through it at random, and as I read the precise, non-figurative prose, even when I didn't understand it, I heard an inner voice checking off the sentences with a Yes. "God—in other words, a substance consisting of infinite attributes, each of which expresses eternal and infinite essence—necessarily exists." "Whatever is, is in God, and without God nothing can be or can be conceived." "He who clearly and distinctly understands himself and his emotions loves God; and the more he understands himself and his emotions, the more he necessarily loves God." "He who loves God cannot wish that God should love him in return." "The love of a thing consists in the realizing of its perfection." "The mind's intellectual love of God is part of the infinite love with which God loves Itself." And finally, at the end of Part 5, "If the way I have pointed out as leading to this result seems exceedingly difficult, it can nevertheless be found. It must indeed be difficult, since it is found so seldom. For if illumination were readily available and could be found without great effort, how is it possible that it should be neglected by almost everyone? But all things excellent are as difficult as they are rare."

As I read, my body began to tingle with an excitement that was hard to distinguish from fear. I looked down at the carpet; it was miles away. I felt as if I had unconsciously rubbed an Aladdin's lamp of a book and instantaneously been transported to the top of a mountain peak by some reckless, too-literal genie. The air was so pure it was almost unbreatheable. A stiff wind whistled through my bones.

Letting go of a merely personal God was difficult, dizzying at first, but it came to be a small pre-taste of freedom. In the fall of 1972, just after my book was published, I began to study the Upanishads, in the W. B. Yeats translation. From their first lines, they made my heart stand up and clap its hands: "That is perfect. This is perfect. Perfect comes from perfect. Take perfect from perfect, the remainder is perfect." These poets knew. They had seen our imperfect, heartbreaking world in its fundamental wholeness, from the place of pure being. They spoke of the Self that is beyond life and death, the Spirit that is everywhere and nowhere, the God that is you and me and the yellow bird on the green branch.

I moved on to the Bhagavad Gita, as Thoreau, another of my American heroes, had done a century before. The Gita was stunning in its depth, its tolerance, and its beauty. "In whatever ways people worship Me, I welcome them. By whatever path they travel, it leads to Me at last." "I am the Self seated in the heart of all beings." But it was especially the eleventh chapter that resonated through and through me. How could it not have? It describes Arjuna's vision of Krishna in His supreme form, with the infinite universe inside him, faces, eyes, limbs everywhere, all creation and all destruction blazing forth from Him with such vast non-moral power that Arjuna, trembling, his hair on end, mute with awe, says, "No more, no more." I knew that place.

After just a few months of reading these texts, I realized that the understanding which shone through them with a light brighter than a thousand suns could not be gained through reading. No words on the page, not even the magnificence of *Job*, not even the profundity of the Gita, would give it to me. I would have to meet the understanding embodied, in the flesh. So I stopped reading entirely. I decided not to begin again until I had some tiny glimpse of the truth. In the spring of 1973 I enrolled in an elementary Hindi course at UC, my intention being, with Elizabeth's concerned permission, to go to India and find a teacher. But before I had learned much more Hindi than "Where is the nearest Western-style bathroom?" the trip to India became irrelevant. Right there in Berkeley, as if by magic, a Zen Master appeared.

3

I heard about Sumi-sahn from my friend George. George had been a classmate of mine at Harvard, where he'd studied anthropology; then, because his interest in Native American ritual, peyote, and large snakes couldn't be accommodated by academic research, he had dropped out, roared off to the Bay Area on his monster black Harley, and set up shop as a carpenter. He was a bright fellow, George, not easily bamboozled. So when he told me that there was a Korean monk in town who was worth checking out, my ears perked up. He said I might even save myself the plane fare to India. The only actual facts he knew about Sumi-sahn were that he was the abbot of a large monastery south of Seoul, that he had come to America six months before, at the age of sixty-three, with no English and a hundred dollars in his pocket, and that he'd been earning his keep repairing washing machines in a north Berkeley laundromat. George also told me that he had once given Sumi-sahn a tab of LSD as an experiment. Sumi-sahn had accepted it ("Oh, special medicine," he'd said), popped it into his mouth, and gone about his business for the rest of the day without any discernible change in consciousness.

He lived and taught in a small apartment in one of the poorest sections of Berkeley. When I knocked on the door, no one answered. That seemed appropriate for a Zen Master, I thought; it didn't necessarily mean that he wasn't in. I decided that, rather than cool my heels in the hallway, with its peeling paint and questionable smells, I would take a walk around the block. Around several blocks.

Before I'd gone on my reading fast, I had dipped into a couple of books on Zen by the Japanese scholar D. T. Suzuki. The explanations were clear and inviting enough. But what really intrigued me were the many dialogues of the old Chinese Zen Masters that Suzuki quoted. They were weird, more baffling than anything I'd ever read, and at the same time compelling. The moment I thought I'd caught a glimpse of meaning, it would be gone. The dialogues kept doing a back-and-forth dance between nonsense and profundity, like the drawing of a human profile that is also, with the slightest shift in perspective, the edge of a goblet.

> Yün-yen was sweeping the ground. Tao-wu came up to him and said, "You look awfully busy."
> Yün-yen said, "There's someone who is not busy."
> Tao-wu said, "If so, there's a second moon."
> Yün-yen thrust out his broom and said, "Which moon is this?"
> Tao-wu turned and left.

When San-sheng first went to see Te-shan, he approached the Master and bowed. The Master said, "What do you want? How dare you think you can stay here and sponge off us? There isn't even a scrap of food here for the likes of you."

San-sheng said, "That's exactly what I thought. If there were any food for me here, I wouldn't have come."

The Master took his staff and hit San-sheng. San-sheng grabbed the end of the staff and pushed him over. The Master burst out laughing. San-sheng exclaimed, "Merciful heavens! Merciful heavens!" and left.

As impenetrable as the dialogues seemed, I found myself falling in love with these old Chinese Zen Masters. I could sense a wildness in them that I had never known in any saint or sage in our Western traditions, and an exhilarating freedom. At about this time I also discovered an ink drawing, in a book of Zen art, that perfectly illustrated my sense of them. It was a drawing of a monk standing upright on the palm of a huge human hand that seemed to be rising in the air. His arms were outstretched in pure exuberance or pure embrace, and he was screaming for joy like a kid on a roller-coaster.

I returned to the apartment after twenty minutes and knocked on the door. Still no answer. I knocked again, much louder, until my knuckles stung. There was a distant "Come in."

The room I entered had seen better days. Cracks in the plaster, loose bricks in the fireplace, buckling floorboards. Everything was neat and clean, but the room itself looked on the verge of collapse, as if it were being held together by safety pins. There was hardly any furniture: just a desk, a small table with a black telephone on it, and a dozen round black meditation cushions lined up along opposite walls like two rows of sleeping cats.

I walked into the kitchen. Seated at the yellow formica table was a small, rosy-cheeked Asian man with a shaved head. He was wearing a sailor's cap, baggy gray pants, and a white T-shirt with large green letters that spelled "WHAT AM I?" His broad smile was like a bear hug. I began to feel uncomfortable. "Hello," he said. "How are you?"

I didn't know what to answer. Was the question just a polite formality, or was he, as a Zen Master, asking me how I really was? And how could I be accurate in just a few words? And was I ready to open up to someone I didn't even know, whatever kind of Zen Master he might be? Finally, as my silence approached rudeness, he laughed—a full, rich belly-laugh—and said, "You think too much." (I am tidying up his English here, as I will continue to do for clarity's sake. What he actually said was, "You many thinking.")

This stunned me into speech. "My friend George said I should meet you."

"Oh, Georgie," he said. "Yes. Sit down. Have some tea."

There was a pot on the table, beside a large bowl of rice and a large, very pungent bowl of kim chee. I poured myself a cup.

"Barley tea," he said. "Drink."

I looked at him as I sipped. There was something amazing about his eyes, something I had never seen in eyes before. They were unusually bright, for one thing. But there was another quality. What was it? And then a couple of lines from a Yeats poem popped into my mind, lines that describe two Chinese sages carved on a piece of lapis lazuli: as they listen to music and stare upon the tragedy of the world, "Their eyes mid many wrinkles, their eyes, / Their ancient, glittering eyes, are gay." Sumi-sahn's eyes had that same quality. They were ancient, glittering, deeply joyous eyes. They were the eyes of someone who knew. I felt that I could walk straight into them, and keep walking for miles and miles, and at the end of the path I would meet myself.

"Now tell me," he said. "Why have you come?"

"I think I've come because I'm unhappy. It's not that I have anything to complain about, truly. I'm married to a woman I love, I have a good job, good friends. But I don't understand life."

"It will be all right," he said. "You are just homesick for your original home."

"My original home?"

"Yes. Zen is understanding yourself. What are *you*?"

The question shocked me, as if a bucket of cold water had been poured onto my head. At the same time it seemed very funny. I remembered the Caterpillar from *Alice in Wonderland*, smoking his hookah and asking Alice the same question, though in a tone of superb con-descension.

"Well," I said, "I'm a writer, a professor, an American, a Jew, a husband, a lover. Should I go on?"

"You say 'writer,' 'professor.' But you *became* all these things. I am asking, what *are* you?"

"I didn't become an American or a Jew. I was born that way."

"Before you were born, what are you?"

Again I was taken aback. "Umm . . . Something . . . A soul. Okay, I'm *one*."

"Where does *one* come from?"

"From God."

"You say 'one,' you say 'God.' If you make one, it is one. If you make God, it is God. All this is thinking. Descartes said, 'I think, therefore I am.' I don't think, therefore . . . what?"

"Therefore, I am not."

"So without thinking, what are you?"

"Nothing."

"Nothing?" Sumi-sahn leaned over and pinched me on the arm.

"Ow!"

"This is pain. Can 'nothing' feel pain?"

"Okay," I said. "You've got a point."

"I ask you again, what are you?"

I felt stumped. I thought for a while, then shrugged my shoulders. "I don't know."

"Aha!" he said, with a huge smile. "This don't-know mind is *before* thinking. It is your original home. Before thinking, your mind was like a sheet of white paper. Then you wrote down 'writer' and 'professor' and 'American' and 'Jew' and 'good' and 'bad' and 'one' and 'God' and 'nothing.' After thinking, there are opposites. Before thinking, there are no opposites. Things are just the way they are. If you cut off all thinking, you erase all these names and forms and return to your original home. 'What am I?' 'I don't know.' When you keep the great question in your mind, you keep the mind that doesn't know. Don't-know mind is your true self."

"Do you mean that I should try to stop all my thinking?"

"No, no, that is already thinking. Don't-know mind is like the full moon. Sometimes clouds come and cover it, but the moon is always behind them. When the clouds go away, the moon shines. So don't worry about this mind: it is always there. When thinking comes, behind it is don't-know mind. When thinking goes, there is only don't-know mind in the clear sky. You must not be attached to the coming or the going."

"It seems rather self-absorbed," I said. "If I stop thinking, how can I teach my classes or talk to my wife? What about the outside world?"

"Where is inside? Where is outside?"

"I'm inside my skin, and the world is outside it."

"This is your *body's* skin," he said, pointing to my arm. "Where is your *mind's* skin?"

"Well, of course, the mind doesn't have any skin."

"Then where is mind?"

"Inside my head."

"Ah, your mind is very small," he said, bursting into loud laughter. Then, patting my hand: "You must keep your mind big. Someday you will understand that God, buddha, and the whole universe fit inside your mind."

"I don't know about that, but I would be very grateful if you could help me understand. I don't want to enter any kind of nirvana; that seems to me a cop-out. But I could certainly use some peace of mind."

"Nirvana is like an empty mirror," he said. "No good, no bad, no happiness, no suffering, no people, no anything. But you can easily get attached to Nirvana, because it is so peaceful. This is no good, because people need us. When we return to our true selves, everything is clear. Happiness is happiness, suffering is suffering. So when you meet someone who is suffering, you relieve his suffering. When you meet someone who is happy, you are happy together."

"And how do you get to that place?"

"You can't *get* there. It is already here. It is already you. What are you doing nowadays?"

"Oh. I'm studying Hindi. I'm on my way to India to find a teacher."

"It is not necessary to go to India."

"But . . ."

"Wherever you are is the center of the universe. Stay here. I will teach you."

There was an amused incandescence in his eyes, as if someone had just turned up a three-way bulb to its maximum wattage. I heard myself say, "All right."

4

I studied with Sumi-sahn for four years. It was a difficult initiation, especially since I was often away from home on retreat. But Elizabeth saw the changes that Zen training produced in me, and she deeply approved. Besides, she got a kick out of Sumi-sahn. Though Zen wasn't her cup of tea, and she seldom came to the Zen center, she enjoyed hanging out with him when she did come. At first I was rather shocked at how irreverent she could be. But he liked that. He would try to engage her in Zen talk, and she would always refuse to bite. Their dialogues used to end up something like this:

Sumi-sahn: "You are attached to thinking."

Elizabeth: "*You* are attached to *non*-thinking."

Sumi-sahn: "The dog runs after the bone."

Elizabeth: "Phoo."

Sumi-sahn: "I will hit you thirty times."

Elizabeth, extending her arm: "Go right ahead, be my guest."

Sumi-sahn: (Loud laughter).

During the first few months of my training, Sumi-sahn would sit with me at the kitchen table, usually in the mid-morning, when the rest of his half-dozen students were at work or at their university classes, and teach me the basics of Dharma (the Doctrine, the Truth)—Buddhism 101, you might say. He began with the three basic characteristics of all phenomena—imperfection, impermanence, and lack of a separate self—and the Four Noble Truths: that pain is a given in this life but suffering is extra and unnecessary; that suffering is caused by the mind tightening around our experience in fear or craving; that the way out of suffering is to let go of all the clutching and sticking; and the particulars of that way out.

All this was eminently sane and reasonable. It required no belief, only action—which was of course the hard part. I could be as skeptical of the teachings as I wanted, and that wasn't a problem; as a matter of fact, it was part of the method. The Buddha himself had said, "It is proper to doubt. Do not be led by holy scriptures, or by mere logic or inference, or by appearances, or by the authority of religious teachers. But when you realize that something is unwholesome and bad for you, give it up. And when you realize that something is wholesome and good for you, do it."

There was a still deeper level of doubt that Sumi-sahn taught me to use as a tool. He said that if I really wanted to penetrate into the truth, both great faith and great doubt were necessary. Faith in myself and trust that the practice, with all its fierce difficulties, would eventually result in freedom. And doubt of everything that appeared in the phenomenal world and on the mental screen, of all objects and also of the perceiving subject—a doubt that made the Cartesian method seem mickey-mouse, since it blithely assumed the "I" of "I think."

Many people have written about the arrival of the Dharma in America. By now there are a half-dozen books about Sumi-sahn alone, including a fine one by my old friend George called *Flagging Down the Buddha Express*. He describes the funkiness, frustration, and hilarity of those early years of practice, presents some of the clearest of the teaching dialogues, and tells the stories that have since become famous in the young annals of Western Zen: "The President of the Cannibals," "Milkshakes and Marionettes," "Sunbathing in Hell," "The Sesame Sutra," "An Elephant on the Roof," "The Sound of Two Hands Clapping," and "Buddha Up Your Ass,"

70

among others. In all these accounts Sumi-sahn displays the openheartedness and improvisationality that have made his teachings masterworks of bodhisattva jazz—two essential qualities when you consider that most of his hippie students, with their acid trips and casual nudity, must have seemed to him like creatures from another world: fascinating, barbaric, full of potential.

I usually went twice a day to meditate at Sumi-sahn's apartment: mornings from five to seven and evenings from seven to nine. In addition, once a month there was a seven-day group retreat with a tough schedule of twelve hours of meditation a day. And because I was a particularly avid student, with a particularly cluttered mind and florid ego to transform, I often found myself drawn to the pressure-cooker practice of solitary retreats: a thirty-day in the fall of 1973, a grueling seven-day full-prostration marathon in 1974 that left my ankles and my libido in shreds, and from 1974 to 1976 three separate hundred-day mantra retreats. During one of these, my tepee retreat, I had a brief, devastating glimpse of angels. More about that later.

I don't need to describe at length what several distinguished American poets and novelists have described so well: the initial phase of meditation practice, which Sumi-sahn used to call "dry-cleaning the mind." The physical obstacles—white-hot pain in the knees, aching back, bone-deep exhaustion—diminished over the months and years until they were familiar background presences, like a neighbor's radio blaring out the kind of music that you detest, then merely dislike, then tolerate with a grudging composure, then eventually, almost affectionately, come to accept. The mental obstacles are even more severe: the shock of discovering how savage and unruly the raw mind is, as if you thought Olivier would be appearing on your mental stage and instead you find a hundred clones of Robin Williams; the interminable boredom of being cooped up with your own random thoughts with no possibility of escape, proving to you at every moment the accuracy of Pascal's diagnosis about the source of all human misery being our inability to sit still in a room; the frustration of seeing and hearing the same neurotic scenarios played out over and over, ad nauseam; the pain of discovering forgotten hurts, envies, and resentments waiting, in suspended animation, for you to come by, like branch-perched rainforest ticks that drop onto a passing animal at the first distant smell of blood; the sense of your own selfishness, which intensifies as your vision grows more clear: not remorse at your own unkindnesses or things you have willfully done to hurt others, but the searing self-awareness that precedes remorse, a sense of mortification so acutely painful that you don't know how you will manage to keep living inside your skin. When I look back at these difficulties from my present vantage point, I am impressed that anyone lasts in the intensive training for more than a few months. But truly I had no choice.

During the first two years of practice I had, as well, a few blessed glimpses of clear mind, when the thick clouds parted and there was a flash of blue sky. But very few. Meditation was the hardest work I had ever done. The difficulty isn't proportional to your intelligence but to your intellectuality. You need to make a sustained effort in order to learn effortlessness, and most of it is a process of unlearning. I had to chip away at the structures of my upbringing and of my Harvard education, then move in with sledgehammer and dynamite. Students who came to the practice with simpler minds had a much more pleasant time of it.

Sumi-sahn was extremely generous with his teaching. I hung out with him most weekday mornings if I didn't have classes. We would sit at his kitchen table, or take long walks, or study a Dick-and-Jane English-for-foreigners textbook I had bought him (my attempt to teach him the subject/verb/object pattern was a resounding failure, as his by now many thousands of students across America and Europe can testify), or go shopping for vegetables at Monterey Market, or sit and drink tea at a café on Telegraph Avenue, or visit one or another of the local churches, where he would sometimes lure an unsuspecting clergyman into a dialogue about God. Time and again he would point out mind-loops in which I was investing huge amounts of energy in thinking about some past or future event that was beyond my control. "Don't check your own mind," he would tell me when I was analyzing myself or trying to gauge my progress. His other constant motto was "Don't check other people's minds." This he would say whenever I was spinning my wheels trying to figure out people's motives. It was incredibly helpful advice. Simplify, simplify. Of course, hearing helpful advice over and over could be annoying. "You always say the same thing," I once snapped at him. He answered, "That's because you never hear it."

As my training progressed, I became more and more

fascinated with the dialogues of the ancient Chinese Zen Masters, which Sumi-sahn would often quote. I couldn't see how they were related to suffering and the end of suffering. There was something at their core that was not present, or at least not obvious, in the serene, rational, transparently clear teachings of the Buddha. I could hear a laughter inside them, rippling through them like light through crystal, from answers that didn't seem at all like answers, but rather like insanely oblique hellos or goodbyes, as if each question were a banana peel aspiring to be a bridge. The laughter was eons upon eons old. It seemed to be coming from the heart of the universe. But what was so funny? How could anyone look upon human life, with all its heartbreak and suffering, as a comedy? I kept straining to understand, but I always felt like some dull clod at a brilliant party, who again and again stands bewildered while the whole room cracks up at a joke and he alone doesn't get it. I knew they had no intention of shutting me out, I could sense how courteous they all were and how stunningly kind, with their twinkly-eyed Chinese faces of crinkled parchment, their shaved heads and blue-green robes. But where was the entrance to that laughter? I wanted to join in, to see the point of it all, to fathom the *hows* and *whys* of my human grief, to fill myself with the spirit's exaltations and cry out with joy in the night, to unravel my karmic knots until I was so spacious that I could swallow the universe in one gulp, and the laughter would be inside me, and just the laughter would be, with nothing outside, with no one laughing.

Many of the dialogues ended with the echo of a grand

explosion—"Upon hearing these words, he was enlightened" or "his mind opened" or "he became intimate." I thought about enlightenment all the time. What could the marvelous insight be? What would it feel like to find yourself beyond sorrow and, even more strangely, beyond joy? Was that even something I wanted? But it was. It was.

Sometimes I would question Sumi-sahn about enlightenment. He would usually smile and say, "Don't make enlightenment." Occasionally he would be more expansive. Once, I remember, I asked him the difference between a mystic and a Zen Master. "A mystic wants to see God," he said. "He wants love, love, love. He wants to develop a special mind. All this wanting is not good, not bad. But it is *making* something. Desire means suffering. Originally your mind is like a glass of clear water. If you add sugar, you have sugar water. If you add salt, you have salt water. If you add shit, you have shit water. But originally the water is clear. That is why Zen Master Nan-ch'üan said, 'Everyday mind is the Tao.' When you stop making everything, mind returns to itself and becomes very simple and clear. Then, whatever you see, whatever you hear, whatever you taste or touch, is the truth."

One morning after meditation practice, I asked him, "What is love?"

He said, "I ask *you*: what is love?"

I couldn't come up with an answer.

"This is love," he said.

Silence. I was waiting for something more.

"You ask me: I ask you," he said. "This is love." It took

me months to get the point of his answer. When I finally did get it, I felt overwhelmed with gratitude.

Among the texts that we chanted every morning and evening before meditation practice was the Bodhisattva's Vow (bodhisattva meaning "enlightenment-being," the person who, having awakened to his or her true nature, is the embodiment of skillful compassion). The vow reads: "Sentient beings are numberless; I vow to save them all. Attachments are inexhaustible; I vow to uproot them all. Dharma gates are everywhere; I vow to enter them all. The buddha way is unattainable; I vow to embody it fully." One morning after practice, a pretty young woman who used to come every day, rain or shine, a student at UC whom I hadn't spoken to more than a couple of times over the months, asked if we could walk to the university together, and on the walk confessed that she was in love with me. In my embarrassment, I said that it was just a crush and she would soon get over it. The next day Sumi-sahn called me into the kitchen. He had heard the young woman's tearful report and was furious. "What kind of bodhisattva are you?" he said. "If you can't save this one girl, how will you save all beings?" This confused and hurt me at the time. I thought that he was being unreasonable, that he was demanding too much of me. But it's hard to stay upset at someone whose rosy, wrinkled, perpetually cheerful face makes him look like the oldest of the elves in Santa's Asian workshop. And in spite of myself, that sentence kept resonating inside me for years.

I never told him about my vision through Hitler's eyes. The reason, I suppose, is that I was overwhelmed by the sheer volume of inner work I had to do, and I felt un-ready to take up this issue just then. Only once did I ever ask him about evil. "Why does shit smell so bad?" I said, apropos of nothing in particular. "If you were a fly," he answered, "it would taste like candy." I didn't continue the dialogue, then or later. Nor could I grasp the essence of what he had said. In fact, it irritated me. But it was the kind of irritation that an oyster might feel when the right grain of sand penetrates its comfortable, water-tight shell.

By the autumn of 1976 my mind had grown clearer and I felt more at peace. There were occasional periods in my meditation practice, after I had acquired enough of the momentum of motionlessness, when very little hap-pened in my mind. Only blue sky. Then there might be a sound—a car, a bell, somebody coughing—and it would appear as pure sound, without triggering a series of asso-ciations and thoughts. Or there might be a flash of pain in my knees and I would simply feel it, without resisting or judging it or wishing it away. Or from far in the distance, like a wisp of smoke being blown toward me, a random thought would arrive, and I would watch it slowly come and watch it slowly dissolve into the air. More precisely, there was no "I" watching the various phenomena, there was just the watching: alert, serene, poised like a dancer on the head of a pin. These periods were wonderful. I hadn't known that it was possible to be so happy.

Then, in January, during a seven-day group retreat, I discovered the secret of the Zen Masters. It happened in Sumi-sahn's interview room. There was no fancy explo-sion of my mind, only a small surprised Oh, as if I was noticing something that my eyes had passed over a million times before. It was all so very simple. There was nothing—no *thing*—that I understood, no content to the experience, though if I had been forced to put words to it, I would have said that for the first time I realized that everything in the world is just the way it is. This sounds inanely tautological. But it was a revelation. I felt lighter than air, suddenly freed from the gravity of *must* and *should*. As I looked at Sumi-sahn with tears of gratitude in my eyes, he burst out laughing. "You slow-poke!" he said. "Do you see how easy it is?" And he leaned over and patted me on the knee.

I can look back on this experience calmly now, with great affection. But at the time, I was euphoric, almost unable to contain myself, so intense was my joy at discovering what had been staring me in the face all the time. For a couple of days I was too excited to sleep. I would burst out laughing or crying at the slightest provocation, for no reason at all. It took me a while to settle down.

A week later, Sumi-sahn called me in for a more substantial talk. "What you had was a glimpse," he said. "It is like wiping clean a little spot on a dirty window, maybe the size of a dime. But your insight is still very unclear. You need to do more hard training."

I was still giddy with joy and had to suppress a giggle. "What kind of training?"

"First you will do some koan work. Then I want you to study with someone else."

"Someone else? What do you mean?"

"I know you love me. I love you too. But we do not have enough affinity," he said (I had taught him the word). "My karma road goes here," drawing a line with his finger along one side of the kitchen table, "and your karma road goes here," drawing a line along the other side. "You will not learn much more from me."

"No, no," I said, suddenly heartbroken. "I have a *lot* more to learn from you."

"So I will send you to another teacher. You will like him. His name is David. He is Jewish, too."

5

I first met David Copland, my dear friend and teacher, in July of 1977. It was a while before I came to know his story. But I knew *him* right away.

David doesn't accept more than three students at a time, and since his training requires a commitment of at least ten years, it isn't easy to get in his door. Fortunately, Sumi-sahn sent me to him when he had only one student (an extraordinary woman who has since then become a fierce embodiment of bodhisattva mind). I must have seemed unusually sincere or needy, or perhaps he was intrigued by my background, so similar yet so very different from his own. At any rate, he took me on, after placing a few minor obstacles in my path to test my resolve. I have my defects of character, but lack of resolve isn't one of them.

When we first met, in his bookbinding studio in the Thousand Oaks section of Berkeley, I was immediately struck by his eyes, as deep and beautiful as Sumi-sahn's. The second thing I noticed that morning, in the corner opposite his work desk, was a little gold-painted statue of the Buddha, smiling to himself and sitting, atop a wooden packing crate, on a carpet of dried rose petals. Four reproductions hung on three walls: Matisse's *Nature morte aux oranges*, a luscious, dream-laden Polynesian woman by Gauguin, Dürer's *St. Jerome*, and Tao-chi's watercolor of a bird-watching poet. The room smelled of glue and leather. David was wearing a Rugby shirt and faded jeans; I remember this because he always wears a Rugby shirt and faded jeans. I also remember feeling for a while rather disoriented (no pun intended) talking to a Zen Master with a Caucasian face.

I asked him about his own training with Zen Master Tao-shan in Japan, and about his great enlightenment in 1962. "Why should you bother about other people's experiences?" he said. "You can find many stories like mine in the old Zen records, but none of them will help you. Ask me a question that really matters."

"What is buddha?" I said.

"Give me a break."

"What is enlightenment?"

"No," he said. "We can throw Zen balls back and forth until we drop. Show me where you're really stuck."

"Ah, stuck," I said. "I'm not sure if I'm ready to get into that just yet."

"If you're not ready for that, you're not ready for the training. What do you think Zen practice is about, anyway?"

"Understanding the truth."

"'Develop a mind that abides nowhere,' the Diamond Sutra says. That's the long and short of it."

"Yes, but aren't there attachments that you shouldn't force yourself to give up all at once?"

"Maybe. But I'm not running a kindergarten here. It's not my job to blow your nose and make peanut-butter sandwiches for your lunch box. To study Zen, you have to want freedom more than life itself."

"I did have a glimpse, you know. But it's not very clear yet."

"Oh?" he said. David's voice had a way of raising its eyebrows. "What's the good news?"

I stood up and slapped him on the cheek.

He laughed, almost inaudibly. His laughter wasn't earthy like Sumi-sahn's. It was subtler than that: air and fire.

"Not bad," he said. "But the next step is crucial. Come back when you're ready to work."

It took me three months to return. I realized that I would have to tell David my Hitler story. I was not looking forward to it.

When I finally gathered myself together and went to see him, he greeted me with *"Barúkh ha-bá,"* which is Hebrew for "Blessed is he who comes (in the name of the Lord)." This seemed incongruous, almost ludicrous, coming as it did from a man who looked and dressed like a Berkeley hippie. It touched me, though. The Hebrew made me feel more seen, more welcomed. But I knew that I was entering the lion's den, and that even if the lion was Jewish and had my best interests at heart, I was going to end up on the ground, as dinner.

I told David about my vision nine years before. I told

him about the horror and shame of the aftermath, the years of searching, my study of the Book of Job and of Spinoza, the Upanishads and Arjuna's vision, my training with Sumi-sahn, the hundred-day retreats, and the very minor opening of my inner eye, a micro-enlightenment, you might say. He listened to me without a word.

When I had finished, he said, "That's enough for now. I'd like you to come back in a week and tell me everything again."

"Again?"

"Yes. You won't find it so hard next time."

He was right. The second time around, I felt less ashamed, more comfortable in my nakedness. The third week, I even felt, at odd moments during the retelling, a little bored. On all three occasions, David said nothing, except to invite me back.

The fourth time was different. "Let's sit outside," he said once I had finished. We walked into the small yard behind his studio and sat down at a redwood picnic table with four redwood chairs around it. The center of the yard was paved with pale yellow bricks. There was a border of azaleas, campanulas, and forget-me-nots around it, with two rose bushes in the north corners. A small but enthusiastic lemon tree stood near the redwood fence.

"You haven't come here to solve the problem of evil," David said. "Someday you may see the answer. But that isn't your job now. Your job is to open your heart."

"Easier said than done."

"Bullshit. You're not even saying it clearly. Once you can say it, you can do it."

"What am I not saying?"

"Two questions have been gnawing at you all these years. The first is 'Why does God allow evil to happen?' The second is 'How can this evil be in me?' Both questions are figments of your imagination. I would like you, for starters, to take a vacation from the word 'God.' Don't say it. Don't think it."

"Why?"

"'Why' is another word I'd like you to chuck for a while."

"Why? Ah ... Hmm."

"God-language may be appropriate as an expression of devotional states. But it's very seductive, and for us it comes with three thousand years of delusion packed into it. There is no Supreme Being out there. You already understand that."

"Granted," I said. "But how does that help me?"

"It simplifies your problem. You don't have to think your way into the mind of God or be involved in the whole rat's-nest of love and anger that your friend Job is stuck in."

"But the love and anger were his way *into* the Whirlwind. God appeared to him because he wasn't afraid to express all of it."

"God has already appeared to you," he said. "You just don't realize it. We are shortening the path by clarifying the love."

"I guess I don't understand how."

"Look: Buddhist practice goes right to the core of the problem. When you understand yourself, your heart naturally opens. It's a very powerful technology."

"I know."

"Have you done any koan work with Sumi-sahn?"

"Yes. I passed through a hundred koans."

"Well, the problem of evil seems to be your natural koan. Life has handed it to you on a silver platter. You can't solve it by thinking. And you are in a very creative place of stuckness, just as Zen Master Wu-men described it seven hundred years ago: the problem is like a red-hot iron ball in your gullet, which you can't swallow and can't cough out. I want you to zero in on this. Sometimes the illness has to get worse before it gets better. You'll be very uncomfortable for a while. Is that okay with you?"

"I think so."

"Good. You were granted a peek under the curtain, long before you were mature enough to deal with it. 'If I rise to heaven, I meet Thee; if I lie down in hell, Thou art there.' You just need to integrate what you've seen."

"Just."

"Listen," he said, "this is very important work. You're doing it not only for yourself. You're doing it for all people, and first of all for Jews."

"But the work seems so un-Jewish."

"Is *Job* un-Jewish? Is Spinoza? They are the glories of the Jewish tradition. They go as deep as you can go on that path."

"I know, I know. But I still feel a conflict."

"But what can be more Jewish than seeking wisdom? Or would you rather spend your life agonizing over agony, as our official Holocaust spokesmen do? What purpose does that serve? 'Never again'? We all hope so. But to wallow in outrage and distrust doesn't help anyone."

I sighed. I remembered once, as chairman of a welcoming committee, driving Elie Wiesel to a lecture he was giving at Harvard. He had tried to convince me that the epilogue to *Job*, in which Job gets his wealth back and brand-new children and lives happily ever after, was an obscene cop-out. I had felt stupid but unconvinced.

"It's such a pity," David said. "Ideas of God are partly at fault here too. God is either all-powerful or all-good, in the traditional theological dilemma. You can't have it both ways, however subtle your reasoning may be, and these people do make the honorable choice, the one that eases their sympathetic Jewish hearts."

"Yes," I said, "I know that attitude. Why do bad things happen to good people? —well, God is doing His best. He truly wants everyone to be happy, but there are things that even a loving God can't fix. He needs our help. Maybe together we can clean up the streets."

David smiled. Then he said, "The whole question is false when you state it as 'Why does God allow evil?' Noun-verb-noun. But the problem isn't theological. It's human. There is no Supreme Being standing outside the universe and allowing anything. And there is no evil."

"How can you possibly say that?"

"We get caught up in such a huge metaphysical dilemma when we use that name. But when we look at our situation more clearly, we see that what we call 'evil' is simply selfishness and the result of selfishness, clinging and the result of clinging."

"But why is there such appalling cruelty in the world?"

"That's simply the way things are. The *why* is in your

mind, not in the world. There's a whole spectrum of possibilities available to humans, from the absolute zero of self-absorption and heartlessness to the point on the thermometer where the self burns up and the bodhisattva heart shines without obstruction."

"The way things are. You're not saying that we should just accept cruelty . . ."

"Of course not. But the best thing we can do for others is to step out of ourselves. When we put an end to our own suffering, we become completely available to help other people put an end to theirs."

"So the less selfish we are, the less we suffer."

"True, in the long run."

"In the short run, though, you have the suffering at Buchenwald and Auschwitz, millions of ordinary people, not any more or less selfish than their Gentile counterparts, while the Nazi sadists live high off the hog and get away with genocide."

"'Why do the wicked prosper?' I realize how hard it is for you not to live inside that question. But give it a rest. Trust me on this. Eventually, you'll understand. Then the question, and the answer too, will disappear."

"I'm not sure I *want* it to disappear."

"You do. Believe me. And then your understanding will be a gift to everyone, including the six million."

"Do you really understand the Holocaust?"

"What I have seen into at some depth are the intricacies of karma. Every cause has an effect, and every effect has a cause. The intelligence of the universe is vast and fierce and absolutely pitiless and absolutely loving, as

86

Arjuna learned in his vision. It made his hair stand on end. Most people who ask 'Why me?' would be terrified to find out the answer. That takes a great deal of courage. Humankind can't bear very much reality."

I sighed again. It was very difficult to see what David was pointing to.

"The web of interconnections is wider and subtler than you can possibly imagine," he said. "It's a dizzying experience when you first look beneath the surface of physical events and start to sense their origin. By now I can see down fairly deep."

"Is there a specific answer for the Holocaust?"

"What's important for you to understand is that at every moment of your life—at every moment—there is absolute justice. This realization is harder for someone who has undergone great suffering. But it's possible."

"I wish I could believe that."

"It doesn't matter whether you believe it or not. Do you know the commandment for Purim?"

"Of course. According to the Orthodox, God commands us to get drunk."

"To get *so* drunk that we can't tell the difference between 'Blessed be Mordechai' and 'Cursed be Haman.' In other words, between 'Blessed be Wallenberg' and 'Cursed be Hitler.'"

"That gives me the willies."

"Because you've been there. There's no going back. You just have to penetrate further."

"How?"

"I'm going to give you a koan to work on. Here's the

text. Memorize it." He opened the book of old Chinese Zen teachings that had fascinated me during the months before I'd met Sumi-sahn, and pointed to a dialogue:

> As Tung-shan and a monk were washing their bowls, they saw two ravens fighting over a frog. The monk said, "Why do such horrors exist?"
> Tung-shan said, "Because of you."

"Oh, great," I said. "That's all I need. The Holocaust is *my* fault."

"No one's talking about fault. The question here is how you hold the cruelty in the world. Cultivate the mind that abides nowhere."

"What should I do specifically?"

"I want you to enter the dialogue as deeply as you can. Sink into it until there's nothing else in the universe. Then see what happens."

"All right," I said. For a few moments I felt too overwhelmed to be polite, then I recollected myself. "Thank you."

"You're very welcome. Come back when you have something to show me."

For five months this practice frustrated me in every possible way. My mind was unruly as it hadn't been since my early meditation days, like a high-strung, skittish stallion being forced into a stall where a rattlesnake is coiled. It would rush off in any direction rather than settle into the contemplation of cruelty. During my formal meditation periods, an hour each morning and evening, I would often get lost in elaborate fantasies for ten or fifteen minutes before I realized that I had wandered from my theme. And I found it impossible to hold the koan in my mind for more than a minute or two during most of my daily activities.

Then, toward the middle of April, something shifted. I was able to enter a state of deep concentration in which the koan remained on my inner screen: troubling, to be sure, but alive. There was minimal static and almost no random thinking. I would pass from the scene into the peace of empty space and back again, apparently without transition. The two seemed like variant modes of the same state, very different from the visionary states of my tepee retreat the year before. There was no ambiguity about what was real. I wasn't inside the scene as an actor; the scene was inside me. My awareness was present in it like the philosopher's God, an infinite circle whose center is everywhere and whose circumference is nowhere.

As I grew more intimate with the koan, every detail became minutely articulated. I could see the two shaven-headed monks washing their bowls in the river after their morning meal of rice gruel and boiled vegetables: the younger one still confused, permeable, searching; the older one, in his fifties, one of the greatest of all the Zen Masters, famous throughout T'ang China for the profundity of his insight and the lightning-quick skill of his teaching words. As they look up, I can see the two ravens and the mangled, half-dead frog. The younger monk shudders and asks his question. The world is so beautiful, the buddha way so clear, and then this cruelty that makes his heart cry out in pain. And what can the Master's response mean? I am just an onlooker. What does this misery have to do with me?

For two and a half weeks his grief and perplexity resonated through my body from morning to night. It was a very precise reflection of my own state of mind, which for six months had been submerged in the joy of my mind-opening. This anonymous monk was my mirror image. The fact that my grief was for millions of human beings and his was for a half-dead frog seemed irrelevant. We were standing in the same place.

And then, just when I was beginning to wonder whether I had sunk deeply enough into the koan to pay David a visit, the focus shifted. I felt my attention being powerfully drawn away from the monk and into another part of the scene. The frog became sharper, more vivid; it grew, as if under a magnifying glass, to twice, five times its initial size. It lay in a heap by the river bank, its flesh shredded, bloody, riddled with holes, one eye pecked out. What remained of it was still feebly trying to escape, but the beaks kept jabbing, tossing it into the air, clamping onto an arm or a leg. The clearer the image became, the more centered I was inside the consciousness of the tortured animal. Eventually I could concentrate so strongly that there was nothing but pain and terror and the jabbing beaks.

At this point I went to see David. "Have a seat," he said. "How's it going?"

"I think I've entered the koan," I said.

"Show me."

I collapsed onto the floor, writhing. "Aaaghhhhh!"

David waited for me to finish, then to pick myself up and sit back in the chair. "No," he said. "Not like that. Go work on it some more."

I was disappointed. I had always been a good student, and my ego felt bruised by his curt rejection. I knew that this was just psychological debris, and that it would flush itself out as long as I remained conscious of it, without judgment. But it was unpleasant to feel. And I was disappointed that I hadn't understood.

The next two months were very difficult. I tried to immerse myself even more deeply in the frog's pain. I could do that for a while, but then my attention would begin to wander. There were times (not long or many) when the practice seemed futile. At times I felt supremely ridiculous. Here I was, sitting on a cushion like an idiot, merging my consciousness with a stupid frog's: and not even a real frog, but a frog in a story. Occasionally my thoughts wandered into a Holocaust scene, and I would feel ashamed, as if the practice, in making my mind equate, even for a moment, the dimly conscious, physical pain of an animal with the prolonged suffering of six million murdered human beings, were an act of blasphemy. Then my shame would pass, and I would find myself immersed in the sorrow of Anne Frank at Belsen, or in the terror of a little Jewish boy in a Nazi photo, his hands held above his head, a blond soldier pointing a rifle at him and grinning in the background, or in the anguish of an old Hasid surrounded by SS troops, one of whom is gleefully ripping out his beard. For a whole week during June, I had to force myself, every morning and every evening, to sit down on my meditation cushion, and had to keep forcing myself to stay. Each hour of formal practice felt like a year. I was sorely tempted to stop meditating entirely, or at least to go and ask David for a practice that was a little more humane. These fits of resistance were intense. Elizabeth would sometimes find me stomping around the house, muttering obscenities to myself. "Koan trouble?" she'd say. I would respond with a "Grrrrrr."

July was a little easier. I was able to stay centered in the frog's consciousness without much interference. I tried not to try so hard. I knew that if I forced myself into the pain, there would be a backlash of distaste and distraction. I tried to let the sinking-in happen by itself. Little by little, it seemed, I was getting deeper. Or I wasn't getting deeper. Maybe I was going nowhere at all. I realized that I had fallen, with a vengeance, into checking my mind. But I couldn't help it.

On the morning of August fifth, to my great surprise, the focus shifted again. Suddenly I was one of the ravens. I felt a fierce hunger, a fierce exhilaration. I rushed to the frog, pecked at the mangled flesh, my heart pounded with the thrill of killing, I grabbed a leg and pulled as the other raven grabbed an arm. A yell of triumph rose from my belly and out my throat. *Caw! Caw caw caw!*

For a moment, I popped out of the raven and back into the frog, then out again as a neutral observer of the scene. A verse from *Job* appeared at the bottom of the screen, like a subtitle in a foreign film: *Who provideth for the raven his food?*

This was too much for me. My body began to tremble, my breath came too fast. I had to stop.

I was too upset to meditate that evening, but I sat down anyway. A wave of fear and disgust washed over me as soon as I crossed my legs in the lotus posture. There I was again, inside the raven, *as* the raven. This time I could taste frog meat in my mouth.

After the long hour was over, I considered my situation. I knew I was at an impasse. One option would be to give up the practice for a while. Maybe it was just too hard for me now. I could stop and take it up later, in a year or two. This might be the prudent course of action. On the other hand, it felt cowardly. Rather than backing up to give myself more room, I could advance to give myself less: maybe room wasn't what I needed. Why not, as revolting as the prospect seemed, plunge further in? I decided to take the next Sunday and meditate straight through for twenty-four hours.

At six in the morning I began. I soon found myself merged with the consciousness of one of the ravens. When I wasn't there, my mind was empty and alert. Occasionally I would enter the frog or the monk, then pop back into the raven, then disappear into the blue sky of don't-know mind. By the end of the day, at six the next morning, I understood what David was trying to teach me. I could enter the raven without judgment, and stay there with as much ease of mind as in any other part of the scene. There was no sense of aversion or struggle.

After two days of rest, I went to see David.

"Well?" he said.

I nodded.

"Show me."

I leaped out of the chair, flapping my wings and caw-
ing at the top of my lungs, then danced around and
around the frog, slashing at it with my cunning beak.
When I sat back down my throat was raw. I was pumped
with adrenaline, and breathing hard.

"Good," David said. Then, after letting me catch my
breath, "Now tell me, how do you see Tung-shan here?"

"How do I *see* him?"

"Yes. Show him to me."

"Hmm."

"No hesitating. Come back when you can show me."

I returned the next day. "Okay," David began. "When
Tung-shan says, 'Because of you,' how do you see him?"

"'Because of you,'" I said, looking at David as if he
were the young monk, feeling my heart open in compassion and a fiery amusement.

"Express that another way," David said.

"'How are you holding your mind?'"

"Or . . . ?"

"'Don't think about it, just look!'"

"A bit harsh."

"Okay. 'Only to teach you.'"

"Good," he said. Then, after a few moments, "Do you
have any questions about the koan?"

"No, it's clear now. I just have a question about what it
implies."

"Yes?"

"Well, I see that the world is a whole, and that every
single being is an equally valid expression of the whole.

94

The mangled frog, the ravens who torture him, the monk whose heart aches, the Master who looks on in deep compassion for them all."

David nodded.

"But how does this translate into the moral world? Is the rapist equal to the young girl who is raped? Is the Nazi murderer as valid as the murdered Jew? I wouldn't be able to stomach that."

"What do you mean by 'equal'?"

"I know there are no heroes or villains in nature, and that frogs and ravens are equal. I guess what I'm saying is that I'd rather be a frog than a raven."

"Is *that* the choice?"

I paused for a few moments. "No," I said. "You're right. I've left Tung-shan out of the equation. But you know what I mean. All men are created equal according to the law, but morally they don't turn out that way. A scumbag doesn't equal a saint."

"Ah, but you see, one aspect of the truth is that we *are* equal. We're all empty, there's no self that you can take hold of, we're all bundles of mind-stuff, and it's important to realize that. The complementary truth is that of course we're anything but equal. Originally we're clear light, all of us, but the more we lose ourselves in selfishness, the more we obscure our essential nature. This moral conundrum of yours is actually very simple. The continuum of being extends from the Buddha, fully conscious and transparent, down to the opacity of the Nazi sadist, who doesn't let *any* light through. That's what we're capable of. It's simply the way things are."

"So what are you saying?"

"Why don't we look at another koan? It goes like this: One day a monk was walking in the garden with Chao-chou and saw a rabbit running away from them. The monk said, 'Master, you are a deeply enlightened man. How could the rabbit be frightened of you?' Chao-chou said, 'It's because I like to kill.'"

"Wow!"

"How do you see Chao-chou here?"

I pointed a rifle, peering down the gunsight, with my left arm held out straight and my right index finger on the trigger. "Bang!"

"How would you express that in words?"

"'Sentient beings are numberless; I vow to save them all.'"

"Yes, of course. Chao-chou was the soul of compassion. He embodied peace as completely as a human being can. It's just that he didn't make separations. If one human was capable of killing, then *he* was."

"But he wouldn't *act* that way."

"That's another story. We're talking about inclusion."

"Well, a Zen Master can afford to be non-judgmental."

"You and I can't afford *not* to be. It costs too much in human suffering. As for Chao-chou, his pure mind didn't divide the world into saints and sinners. As a matter of fact, when a monk once asked him, 'What is the holy?' he answered, 'It's like dumping a mountain of shit on the front lawn.'"

"The point being . . ."

"To throw away all these categories. The world is luminous. The luminosity is you. Once you stop getting caught up in the dramas of good and evil, you can cultivate the mind that abides nowhere."

"Hmm."

I stared at the floor. For a minute or two neither of us spoke. Outside the studio, the voice of a mockingbird rushed up and down its crystal staircase.

"Let's approach the issue from a different direction," David said. "Here's what I'd like you to do next. Have you heard of *metta* practice?"

"Yes. I have friends who trained with teachers in Burma and Thailand."

"*Metta*, you may know, is the Pali word for 'loving-kindness' or, more accurately, 'benevolence.' It's a practice that dates back to the Buddha himself. The old fellow had a lot on the ball. When the mind is happy, he discovered, we naturally wish for the happiness of all beings. Your friend Spinoza expressed the same thing in God-language: 'The good which everyone who loves God wishes for himself, he also wishes for all others; and the greater his knowledge of God is, the greater this wish is.'"

"You've been reading the *Ethics*?"

"Set a thief to catch a thief."

"Ah. Well, I'm honored."

"Spinoza doesn't say that the lover of God wishes well to *most* others, or to all *good* others, but to *all* others. That's the point. Spinoza was as clear as can be about this. But the advantage of the Buddha's teaching is that he handed down a method to cultivate and deepen that mind. It's a practice that would normally precede koan practice. But in your case this is a good time."

"Okay," I said. "I'm game. What do I do?"

It was a simple practice, though more discursive than anything I had been assigned in my training with Sumi-sahn. It consisted of repeating a specific formula of wishing people well, concentrating on the words and letting the feelings come and go. You start out with yourself, since benevolence begins at home. "May I be free of suffering," you repeat into your inner ear. "May I have physical happiness. May I have mental happiness. May my heart be at peace." The point isn't to *feel* benevolent, or loving, or kind, or anything in particular. Feelings are irrelevant. You just repeat the phrases and let the feelings take care of themselves.

The practice was a cinch, at first. I enjoyed hanging out in this meditative space, which had a lucidity to it that was on the other end of the devotional spectrum from the obscure ecstasies of my broccoli-smoking days. Benevolence is a very crisp sensation, actually, like walking along the seashore at dawn. Everything begins to glow with a vigorous, early-morning tranquility. After a while, you aren't aware of an "I" who wishes happiness to a "myself." There is just the lovely, temperate wishing, a radiance without direction or agenda. You feel that your whole body has turned into the smile on the face of the Buddha.

The next two stages of practice were just as pleasant. First, as instructed, I sent *metta* to a benefactor (I sometimes visualized Elizabeth, at other times Sumi-sahn or David). "May you be free of suffering. May you have physical happiness. May you have mental happiness. May your heart be at peace." Mmmm. Giving was receiving. The energy that I sent out returned to me in the same integral, fluid movement. It was the easiest thing in the world.

Then I visualized a neutral person, the bank teller with the mustache and watery eyes or the plump blond girl at the grocery store. Same effortless process. "May you be free of suffering, old man walking your dog, woman sitting on the bench in the park. May you be happy."

The trouble came during the second week, when my instructions were to send *metta* to the Enemy. David had warned me to begin with someone manageable. But I'm a fairly genial person, and I haven't made enemies, at least to my knowledge. There was a classmate at Harvard who hated me for a while because I had a love affair with his former girlfriend, and I'd heard that Professor X, a colleague of mine at UC Berkeley, started badmouthing me after *1672* was praised in *The New York Review of Books*. But I hadn't taken the dislike personally. It seemed absurd, comical, and my main reaction to it had been surprise that someone didn't like me. So wishing them well took no effort on my part. As I sat there visualizing them and saying the four phrases, it was easy to keep broadcasting the Buddha's smile over the airwaves of the spirit, although I must admit that occasionally, for a few moments at a time, I noticed the smile flicker into a smirk of self-satisfaction, as if the Buddha had suddenly been reincarnated as the Cheshire Cat.

I knew I would have to move on to Hitler. But when I

tried to concentrate on him, my will power shut down. Complete distraction. Random thoughts tore through my mind. An iron resistance set in. There was no way I could continue with the phrases. Even a tentative motion of my will toward saying "May you be . . ." nauseated me. If I could have let myself express a wish, it would have been "May you suffer as much as you made each of the six million suffer." I didn't go so far as to think the truly horrible "May you burn in hell." But I came close.

For two days I struggled with this meditation for the Enemy. Of course, what I was doing wasn't meditation at all. I just sat there stewing in my own juices. It was excruciatingly uncomfortable. When I couldn't take any more, I paid David a visit.

"You look like shit," he said.

"Thanks. It hasn't exactly been a picnic."

"Hitler?"

"Yup," I said. "My main man."

"That's obviously too much for you right now. There's something to be said for moderation, you know."

"But I don't *have* enemies. And I'd really like to confront this issue. I'm so sick of carrying it around."

"Tell me what's been happening."

I described in detail the misery of the past two days. David nodded his head.

"Let's step back for a while," he said. "I want you to investigate what goes on in your mind when you do the meditation for the Enemy. Just feel what you feel."

"Okay."

"Now."

"Now? Really?" I said. "All right." I tried to think the

first phrase. Immediately everything blocked. There was a fiery energy in my chest area. My heart tensed. I opened my eyes.

"What would you call that?" David said, after I had reported my emotion.

"Rage. And a lot of resistance."

"I would call it hatred."

No, I thought, it couldn't be. But then I caught myself. My God, *was* it hatred?

"This is difficult to hear, I know," David said. "But stay with me. You've got to penetrate this point. Everything depends on it."

There was a sinking in my stomach, as if I were going up in an elevator. I felt like running away.

"Hatred is a mode of suffering. Do you understand that?"

"Yes."

"It's a kind of aversion, the reverse side of craving, which is the fundamental cause of all suffering. When you hate, you cause a contraction of your heart. It's the same kind of emotion as hurt is, except that hurt shrinks inward, while hatred strikes outward at some object. Do you see that?"

"Yes."

"Now follow me. Hatred is Hitler's ruling passion. It fills his mind and poisons it. I don't need to tell you what that feels like. But when *you* hate *him*, you're locked inside that same mind."

"Wait a minute," I said. "That's different. He *acted* on his hatred. He built a whole life on it."

"Of course it's different. But the clearer we get, the

greater the demand for impeccability. What he felt on the grossest level of consciousness, you feel on a subtler level. Hatred moves from the unconscious to the conscious; then, if it's given fuel, from thought into action. That's why the verse in Leviticus says, 'You shall not hate your brother in your heart.'"

"Whoa!" I said. "Hold on now. You're applying that verse to *Hitler*? My *brother*?"

"He's a human being, isn't he?"

"He's a goddamn monster!"

"What about your talismans from Terence and Goethe?"

"Fuck Terence! Fuck Goethe!"

"Stay with me. You need to see this."

"Fuck you!" It spurted out of my mouth before I could catch it. "David, I'm sorry."

"That's all right," he said. "I know how hard this is. But I want you to look more closely. Where does hatred come from?"

"Where does *any*thing come from? From emptiness."

"On a phenomenal level. What underlies hatred? Breathe."

I paused and closed my eyes. Beneath that fiery energy in my chest I could feel . . . "Fear."

"Fear of what?" David said.

"I'm afraid of him. Afraid of any kind of racism. I'm afraid I'll be killed."

"Yes. Beneath hatred there's always fear of harm. You're afraid that Hitler will harm you, Hitler is afraid that Jews will harm him. Ultimately this fear arises from ignorance."

"You're not saying that this is a fantasy on the part of Jews, are you? If I'm a Jew living in Berlin in 1933 or Poland in 1939, I'd goddamn *better* be afraid."

"Don't fly off to Berlin. Stay with me here. We're not talking about the fear that's an animal response to danger, like when your car is going off the road. Even a buddha would feel that. We're talking about basic ignorance. Ignorance of the way things are."

"Well, yes, I understand that. Ignorance gives rise to craving or aversion. We think that if only we can get some object, or push some object away, we'll be happy. That's the beginning of all our trouble. I'll grant you that. Hitler was dangerously ignorant. All the involved racial theories, all the fear and aggression came from that darkness."

"And what would you say is the appropriate response to someone else's ignorance?"

"David, I beg you, don't make me say this."

"How would a bodhisattva respond?"

I sighed. "The appropriate response is compassion. Do I get an A?"

"When you can say it, you can do it."

"But I refuse to forgive him. That would be asking too much."

"It's not a question of forgiveness," David said. "Forgiveness is a path to inner freedom. But a wrong that's not done to you isn't yours to forgive. That's why I'm taking you on the path of benevolence. Hatred is a kind of clasping. You've been carrying Hitler around in your mind for ten years now. It's time to let go."

"If only."

"Why do you think you were granted the vision through Hitler's eyes? That mind is inside you too. It's a possibility latent in every one of us. In Jewish terms, it's the unconscious part of God's mind, the dark corner of paradise. Your job is to go back and walk through it like Rabbi Akiba, in peace."

"How?"

"Just be present. Hatred, anger, grief, fear, whatever you are feeling—just see it clearly, without judgment. Let it come and go, and realize that it's okay."

"So I should stop the *metta* practice?"

"Yes. Later on, you'll come back to it, and after that, we'll do advanced koan work. But I want you to have a deeper clarity first. Good luck."

I practiced *vipassana*, insight meditation, for a year. It was a long year. I spent a lot of time painfully inhabiting my hatred and fear. In the light of intense awareness they began to diminish. By the end of August, 1979, they had mostly disappeared.

David monitored my progress very closely. When he put me back on *metta* practice in early September, he said, "Take it lightly. And here's another talisman for you, from the twentieth-century Jewish mystic Rav Kook: 'It is our right to hate the actions of an evil man, but because his deepest self is the image of God, it is our duty to honor him with love.'"

"That's wonderful."

"It's not that there's no distinction between pure and impure. But we are all created equal, and even in the most degraded among us, even in Hitler, the innocence

we come from is still alive. Beneath all our pain and ignorance and unsatisfied desires, it shines with its pristine
light, as it did in the beginning."

"Ah."

"Here's how I want you to start the practice again. I'd
like you to visualize a circle of sages: Spinoza, Chao-
chou, Tung-shan, the *Job* poet, anyone else you love and
admire. Visualize yourself sitting in the center. Then
have them send you *metta*. 'May you be free of suffering.
May you be happy.' After you've done that for a few days,
I want you to bring Hitler into the center of the circle,
and have the sages send *metta* to *him*. See what happens."

It turned out to be easy. I could feel the waves of benevolence washing over him, over me. But when, at the end
of a week, I tried to repeat the phrases as myself, I still
couldn't say them with conviction.

"Let's be more gradual," David said. "Can you say to
Hitler, 'May you be free of hatred'?"

"Yes," I said. "That sounds doable."

I sent *metta* to him in this mode, without a problem,
for two weeks. Then David moved me on to "May you be
free of the suffering of hatred." By the middle of October
I was able to say "May you be free of suffering" and mean
it. I can't describe the joy of this meditation. I felt that an
enormous burden had been lifted from my heart. By the
third week of December I had expanded my meditation
to include all beings, in all dimensions, the large and the
infinitesimal, the good and the wicked. "May you be free
of suffering. May you have physical happiness. May you
have mental happiness. May your heart be at peace."

On January third, on the fifth day of a seven-day retreat, at four-thirty in the afternoon, I suddenly found myself in the center of *Job's* Whirlwind. I saw—not understood but *saw*, with my own eyes—that there is perfect justice in the universe, for me, for you, for frogs and ravens, for Hitler, for the six million, for all beings. It doesn't happen later, in some otherworldly reckoning. It isn't later, but always now. This was not a thought. It flashed through my body like lightning. Everything became perfectly lucid. It was so simple that I gasped. Then I laughed out loud. The whole universe laughed.

When I saw David three days later, I bowed to him—not a full prostration, but a small, tactful, deeply reverent, Jewish-American bow. "Thank you so much."

"You're very welcome," David said. And after a few moments: "Now you can begin the real work."

chAptEr III

aFTER I HAD RECOVERED from my lesson
in angelic sex, I reread *Against Angels*, following Gabriel's
suggestion. It was the first time I'd looked at it since it
had been published three years before. I still liked it,
though naturally it needed to be revised in the light of
that afternoon's visit.

The idea for the book had come to me as I was inspecting a bathroom—my friend Helen's office bathroom, to
be precise. It was a glorious early-November day in 1990,
warm and crisp, the air rich with fermenting grapes.
Having just finished picking apples and hunting out the
last of the walnuts from under their loud-crunching
leaves, I was in a particularly earthy, harvestful mood.
Helen had recently moved her psychotherapy office to

the in-law annex of her house and had remodeled it with her usual effusive attention to detail. Everything was meant to be soothing. "Like a sanctuary," she had told me. Sanctuaries apparently require angel pictures on the wall, angel cushions on the couch, and angel pins stuck in odd corners of the armchairs and bookcase. Helen, I should tell you, is by no means a flake. She's a tough, savvy woman who, in addition to her therapy practice and raising the last of her three kids, works at an AIDS hospice three nights a week, sitting at the bedsides of the dying, holding their hands and talking to them about spirit as their bodies fall apart. I have sat with her. She has a big heart.

The walls were painted a creamy pinkish off-white, the rug was light coral, there were pinks and soft purples in all the angel pictures, the pin-studded upholstery was lavender, with blue and green flower patterns. It stopped just short of being revolting, if indeed it did stop short. A glorified version of a child's bedroom, I thought, though with some effort I could understand how useful such an atmosphere might be for patients sickened with too much adulthood. Forever-gentle, forever-anonymous New Age flute-and-harp music floated down from speakers at the four corners of the ceiling. Was that gurgling accompaniment a porpoise?

I stepped into the bathroom. Pink tiles, pink towels with enamored teddy bears embroidered onto them. There were two framed reproductions on the walls: Leonardo's *Annunciation* and the angel musicians of Hans Memlinc. And on the toilet-tank lid a row of angel books, all the same chunky shape, with pastel covers. I read the spines: *Letters to the Angels, Listening to Angels, Dancing with the Angels, Angels and Avatars, Finding Your Guardian Angel, Angel Prayers, More Angel Prayers*, and finally, as if angels were an exotic variety of hummingbird, *100 Ways to Attract an Angel*.

It was at this point that I was struck by the idea. Actually, it wasn't so much an idea, at first, as a feeling, which surfaced along with the title *Against Angels*. Standing there in the bathroom, alone for a few minutes as Helen ground the coffee beans and set out the muffins, I found myself barely able to contain my exasperation. Here was my dear friend, an intelligent woman, someone not wholly lacking in spiritual insight, who nevertheless had fallen head over heels for what I could only call a sappy fantasm. A dozen questions were bubbling up into my mind, but I didn't want to look at them just yet. What I noticed first was the quality of my annoyance and the obstreperousness that accompanied it. All these angels were making me feel devilish. Part of me had become a four-year-old holding a pin in a room full of balloons. I was Chuang-tzu with a pitchfork, the laughing enemy of the solemn and the pious. I was the belch at high tea with the Duchess of Norfolk, the wad of gum in the Gideon Bible, the firecracker under the podium at the bank president's speech, the red-haired quark that runs zigzag through the great hall of science, I was John Philip Sousa's five-hundred-man brass band marching down the aisles of St. Patrick's Cathedral at the elevation of the Host.

I could hear Helen's voice calling that the coffee was

ready. By the time I stepped out of the bathroom and sat down at the kitchenette table, I had some sense of where I wanted to begin my investigation. But I didn't have a clue about where it would eventually take me.

2

I began the book with an epigraph from Spinoza: "A mouse no less than an angel, and sorrow no less than joy, depend upon God; yet a mouse is not a kind of angel, nor is sorrow a kind of joy." This sentence puzzled some of my readers. It had once puzzled *me*. But profundity often stands on the brink of nonsense, and even before I fully understood Spinoza's insight, I felt that this was a delicious sentence. I used to chew on it for hours.

At the time, I thought that the epigraph, though subtle, was clear enough in expressing the central point that all things return to the One and the One returns to all things; my book was a two-hundred-seventy-eight-page footnote. Besides, its juxtaposition of mice and angels repeated, three centuries before the fact, a juxtaposition that life had handed me during a long and difficult retreat, when mice were my joy and angels my sorrow. If nothing else, it announced that whether or not angels exist in reality (physical or non-physical), they exist in the world of the human mind, even in the mind of the supremely rationalistic Spinoza, that God-intoxicated man, for whom "reality" and "perfection" were synonymous. The important question was *how* they exist. They aren't necessarily characters in a sentimental, Christmas-pageant world, as in conventional Christian or New Age religion. An angel can be pure intellect, pure spirit, as in the philosophy of Aquinas. Or it can be something even greater, in the dynamic of a more mature mind: not a comfort but a challenge, as Rilke's vast, terrifying angel is. Or, reflected in a still clearer mind, it is simply a temporary apparition, just as much an everything and a nothing as any other being is, and all its fascinating beauty is seen as a distraction from the central issue of life and death.

The Zen story I began my fourth chapter with provides the clearest perspective, and makes other encounters with angels seem like kindergarten tales. The story's hero, the monk Yün-chü, is a very talented student, but because he has not yet fully ripened, he's still caught up in the seductive pleasures of the otherworldly. When his mind and heart finally open to the splendor of *this* reality, right here, right now, which contains all possible worlds, he no longer even sees the angels and the angels can no longer see him.

> Yün-chü built a meditation hut on San-feng Mountain. He spent ten days there without walking down to the monastery. When at last he came, Master Tung-shan asked him, "Why haven't you shown up for meals lately?"
>
> Yün-chü said, "I don't need to. Every day angels bring me food. It is most delicious."
>
> "Hmpf!" said the Master. "I thought you were a superior student. Come to my room later tonight."
>
> When Yün-chü entered Tung-shan's room, the Master shouted, "Yün-chü!"
>
> "Yes?"
>
> "Don't think of good; don't think of evil; what is it?!"

Upon hearing this, Yün-chü's mind opened.

When he returned to his hut and resumed his meditation practice, the angels were unable to find him, and after three days they stopped appearing.

This is the quintessential angel story. It says everything that needs to be said. What matter-of-fact skill the ancient Master showed in weaning his student from the unearthly! And with what alacrity the student stepped back into himself! Everyday mind is the Way.

3

As it turned out, the most controversial section of *Against Angels* was the least instructive part to write. This was the first chapter, "Going Ape over Angels," my analysis and—I hope not unkind—critique of the current angel mania. When I say "least instructive," I don't mean that it didn't teach me anything or that I didn't enjoy writing it. It's just that I wasn't all that interested in the *why* of the phenomenon. Mainly, the chapter gave me a chance to express the growing angelogenic irritation I had felt over a number of years and hadn't been fully aware of until that moment in Helen's bathroom. Several times as I discussed the trivialization of spirituality in popular culture, I found myself surfing a tidal wave of annoyance, and these pages were among the best things in the book. I didn't censor them or try to be fair to the New Age or fundamentalist angel people. I simply let loose.

Though I mentioned a few of our more cloying TV and movie angels, my discussion centered on the angel books of the eighties and nineties. Sometimes the passages I quoted were so silly that I let them stand on their own. More often they called for a few choice mephistophelian comments, a low heat underneath them to bring out the full flavor of their absurdity. (I particularly enjoyed plumbing the shallownesses of Billy Graham's *Angels: God's Secret Agents*, a hilariously rectilinear book, with a title that could only have been thought up by someone who had been chummy with presidents and C.I.A. directors.) While I was writing most of this chapter, I imagined Helen sitting in front of me, as she is today but as she looked twenty-five years ago, with her waist-length chestnut hair and dark brown eyes that smoldered with indignation at any hint of corruption or sentimentality. I wrote what in person I couldn't say to her because I didn't have the right to: how foolish this undue interest in angels was, how unworthy of her.

Rereading the chapter now, five years after I wrote it, I was amused by the baroque energy of its exasperation. Had I really needed ninety-eight pages to make fun of angels and angel-watchers? Had the theme required so many dozens of variations, when just three or four would have been enough? Perhaps. I remembered that as I wrote it I'd been particularly pleased with the section called "Diatribe on Cherubs," which traces the degeneration of the cherub image, from the *kerubim* of Genesis—those immense human-headed bulls with eagles' wings who are stationed at the east of Eden to guard the path to the Tree of Life—into the infant-angels of Renaissance paintings and contemporary kitsch. The notorious trial scene at the end of this section, in which I bring the fat, fluttering, rose-cheeked modern cherub to the dock, with Mother Teresa as his doting defense attorney and a wry St. Paul as his prosecutor, still made me laugh. But it *did* seem like breaking a butterfly upon a wheel, as the Washington *Post* reviewer had said.

Nevertheless, although the points could have been made more concisely and with greater tact, they were points, I felt at the time, that needed to be made.

Why angels? I wrote a few pages examining this question. The obvious reason is that most people's spiritual longing fastens upon accessible images, and with traditional images of God becoming more and more threadbare and unusable, the image of the angel is next in line, as the next-highest order of being in the traditional monotheistic universe. It is powerful but not all-powerful. There is nothing threatening about it: no God-the-Frowning-Father or Jesus-the-Righteous-Judge. The angel is all downy wings and shiny smiles, a combination of grandmother and Big Bird. How lovely to be back in pre-adult, pre-scientific consciousness, lying in the dark after the good-night kiss, thinking of those liminal forms that must be thinking of you, floating in a world where fear is kept at bay by the most tender and permeable of babysitters.

It's not that I disbelieved *all* the narratives of angelic rescue that had proliferated over the preceding decade in weekly newsmagazines and pastel-covered angel paperbacks: a very small number seemed to have a kernel of authentic experience in them, however naive their mythological framework was. The vast majority of them, to be sure, were sentimental and self-deceptive. They were carbon copies of Bible stories, with only the surroundings changed. Instead of a tent, a condo; instead of a field, a mall. Invariably they were told not as myth startling into life but as life flattened into myth. One bestselling paperback, entitled *They Came Down from Heaven*, purported to document five hundred cases of angelic appearances in America between 1985 and 1990. Each case was a first-person account, ranging from a single paragraph to three pages long. Case #1: An old woman falls while crossing Second Avenue in Manhattan and is lifted to her feet by two beautiful young men with white wings; one escorts her across, the other picks up her spilled bag of groceries. Case #2: A car skids out of control on a Colorado freeway, almost crashes into a bus, but is stopped just in time by a ten-foot-tall angel who interposes himself with outstretched palms. And so on. Almost all the stories were one-dimensional and didn't call for much comment. They were like narratives of UFO encounters: the more spectacular the details, the more trivial the story.

The final section of this chapter dealt with the image of the guardian angel, especially in our current American version. It's a charmingly democratic idea: why shouldn't every one of us, baptized or heathen, be assigned a celestial bodyguard? Some angel experts even maintain that dogs and cats have their own dog- and cat-angels, and I suggested that it was short-sighted and uncompassionate to stop there, without ascribing guardian angels to sparrows, worms, paramecia, algae, and viruses.

Throughout Chapter One, and especially in this section, I was in what to some readers seemed the uncomfortable position of having to criticize an image as cherished and comforting as Santa Claus. "What is wrong with wanting to feel safe?" people kept asking me on the book tour. "Why shouldn't we teach our children that they are protected, if this very teaching makes them feel protected? What's the big to-do?"

Well, I felt strongly about this. The main problem with the figure of the guardian angel is that it trivializes the idea of safety. Everyone wants to feel safe, of course. But in this life of ours, the feeling that we can be protected by anything—by feathery guardians or by our own goodness or faith or wisdom—is an illusion. Any event can happen to us. Any difficulty, pain, grief, or loss can visit us at any moment; these events we label accidents or disasters, though in fact we often can't know what is good or bad for us. As the great French-Jewish theologian Simone Weil wrote, "Every time we say 'Thy will be done,' we should have in mind all possible misfortunes added together." There *is* no safety, except the ultimate safety: to let go of life and death and realize that there was never anything to let go of.

What I most objected to in the figure of the guardian angel was the sense of the world that underlies it. Do only a few privileged people have guardian angels, while the rest are left to fend for themselves? This seemed to me almost as much of a blasphemy as is the Christian image of a God who separates humanity into the saved and the damned. Or on the contrary, does everyone have a guardian angel? If so, most guardian angels have botched it royally, since for every miraculous rescue there are countless millions of instances in which the angel has been snoozing on the job and there is no rescue.

And where were all the guardian angels during, for example, the Holocaust?

I did not belabor this point.

4

David had enjoyed *Against Angels* when it came out in 1992. He told me I'd done a fine job digging into the subject, especially in the sections on Aquinas and Rilke, and he thought the book would be useful to people in spite of its "Zen stink." "But I had no idea," he said, "that the angel craze pushed your button so strongly."

"Neither did I," I said. "Until I started."

"In hindsight, of course, it's understandable. You spent a lot of time, as a young man, longing for goodness. That left a certain residue. You were searching for something more than human, though all goodness lives in the human heart. It's the reverse side of your fascination with evil. Thank God that phase is over with."

"Amen," I said.

"Anyway, given your annoyance, I think it was a healthy thing to write the book. Do you know the story about the Hasidic rabbi Yaakov Yosef of Podolsk? It's not in Buber's *Tales of the Hasidim*."

"No. Tell me."

"A merchant once approached Yaakov Yosef and said,

'When my neighbor offends me, what should I do with my anger?' Yaakov Yosef said, 'Are you angry *at* him or *for* him?' The merchant couldn't answer. Yaakov Yosef said, 'If you are angry *at* him, your anger is like Balaam's angel, blocking your way: it is better to be an ass than a prophet. If you are angry *for* him, your anger is like Tobias's angel: let it take you by the hand to a country you would never find on your own.'"

"It's true," I said. "'The tygers of wrath are wiser than the horses of instruction.' I followed my anger, and voilà, a book."

"Yaakov Yosef also declared, on another occasion, 'Thinking about angels is like sitting at the king's banquet table, before the first course is served, and stuffing your belly with bread.'"

"I know, I know. I did get a little obsessed. But it was a way of getting angels out of my system."

"If they *are* out of your system," David said.

5

The analysis and critique of America's love affair with angels needed to be made, it seemed to me at the time—and I enjoyed making it. Still, Chapter Two, "The Idea of the Angel," was a greater pleasure to write, because it is a chapter of less irony and more appreciation. In it I set out to consider the traditional worlds of thought in which angels exist, and to understand, where I could, such disparate, polarized, brittle, compelling mind-constructions.

To the psyche, the archetype of the angel, after all, has

nothing to do with God or with messages; it is simply the figure of a human body with wings. As such, it is the focus of a basic human longing. The part of us that dreams of flying wants freedom from all physical limitations and takes gravity as a kind of defeat, feels the pull back to earth as a tragic incapacity to stay in the infinite blue sky. We don't have the same longing to live in fire or water. That's because air is what we breathe, it is our most intimate element, it passes in and out of our bodies, yet our bodies can't fully pass in and out of *it*. We admire and envy birds for being breathed by the air, for soaring and plunging through its veins and currents as we can't; in the sky, the body of a bird becomes pure joy, an emblem of boundlessness, a triumphant banner. Nor has our desire to fly been assuaged in the slightest by the invention of the airplane. We still dream of flying by ourselves, not with wings, but with our whole body. The dreams begin with a sense of coming into our own. Suddenly there is a knowing, the kind of physical comprehension that a child has when for the first time he can keep his balance on his two-wheeler: in a huge exhilaration the body lifts off the ground, the houses grow smaller, and we soar into the freedom of the night sky and think, "Oh; this is how it's done; it's the easiest thing in the world!"

I began Chapter Two, naturally, with the infrequent but famous angel passages in the Hebrew Bible and the Gospels, and proceeded to examine the image of the angel in the Apocrypha and Pseudepigrapha, the Talmud, Midrash, and *Zohar*, the Koran, the equivalent figures in the Hindu, Buddhist, and Taoist cosmologies, and the angels of two great Western poets, Dante and Milton. But most of my discussion in this chapter concentrated on the late antique and medieval Jewish, Christian, and Muslim theologians, since of all the angel literature theirs were the most minute and passionate inquiries.

The speculations that I discussed, briefly or at length, range from the rapturous hymns of cosmic hierarchy by the sixth-century Syrian monk known as Pseudo-Dionysius to the cool Aristotelian ratiocinations of Maimonides, and include the writings of Philo of Alexandria, Origen, Gregory of Nazianzus, Augustine, Gregory the Great, Saadia Gaon, Avicenna, Solomon ibn Gabirol, Judah ha-Levi, Hildegard of Bingen, Averroës, Bonaventure, and especially Thomas Aquinas, the Angelic Doctor, the most comprehensive and meticulous theologian of them all.

I studied Aquinas' angels with particular care because the way that all these discussions move is most clearly discernible through the movements of his very orderly mind. Like other angelologists, he deduced a whole set of qualities from the basic premises that there are such beings as angels (they appear in the Bible, therefore their existence is a revealed truth), that they were created by God, and that they are capable of existing, in heaven and occasionally on earth, wholly in order to serve God and to praise Him. Aquinas had one additional premise, which appears in his work as an eightfold proof: that angels are composed entirely of spirit and not, as Augustine and some of the other theologians maintained, of spirit mixed with a subtle form of matter. From this idea of a purely spiritual being, everything else in his description follows, proved with admirable thoroughness and a strict logic that doesn't begin to show its weirdness until you step outside the system of Christian thought.

Aquinas answered a wide range of questions about the angelic nature and functions. If angels are purely spiritual, how do they interact with matter? When they are visible to humans, as the Bible says they can be, is it only as vaporous apparitions, or do they temporarily inhabit bodies of flesh and blood? Since they are created beings and had a beginning, do they also have an end, or are they eternal? Were they created before the physical universe? When they were created, were they already in bliss, or did they have to earn it? In what way are they superior to human beings? What is the difference between a soul and an angel? Can angels move instantaneously from place to place, or does their movement require time? Can they be present in two places at the same time? What language, if any, do they speak among themselves? Does an angel by nature love God more than himself? Can an angel love one particular angel more than another? Do angels' minds function by means of intellectual powers, or are they wholly intuitive? Can they know the future? (The answer here is, surprisingly, No.) Can they read the thoughts of humans? (Again, surprisingly, No.) Can angels make mistakes? (No.) Do they have free will? (Yes.) Can they grow in blessedness? (No.) Are they capable of sin? (No.)

Hanging out with the angel sections of the *Summa Theologica* turned out to be a curious experience, as maddening at first as it was exhilarating. When, after some effort, I was able to center myself in my intellect and to disregard my body, my emotions, and the rest of me, I could feel a kind of snug pleasure in Aquinas' reasoning, as if I were a cat curled up on a large warm lap. Sometimes this pleasure would intensify to wonder. It was like living beside a huge, translucent, three-dimensional, animate chess game. The beauty and intricacy of the logic was astounding. Everything followed in perfect order from the central premises. The pieces moved right or left or kitty-cornered or up or down; the opponents, actual or hypothetical, Greeks or Jews or heretics or Doctors of the Church, made their justified or mistaken conclusions or objections; and Aquinas corrected and explained it all. If this, then that. If not that, then not this.

During the three weeks when I submitted myself to the discipline of inhabiting Aquinas' thought, of seeing with his eyes and breathing through his nostrils, I came to understand how comfortable the world view of the Church could be. "Just give your assent to a few little preliminary ideas," the *Summa* whispered, "and I will take care of everything else; I will settle all your questions, even the questions you don't know how to ask; I will order the world into a total structure, a magnificent architecture of hierarchically interconnecting ideas. Everything will be decided forever. Let me do it for you. Trust me." I could feel the satisfaction this kind of system provided; at least, for several pages I could feel it. There I was, standing in the downtown of Christian culture, with the great emporiums of belief lining the granite boulevards. Reason and

Revelation strolled arm in arm beside me on a spring afternoon, window-shopping. All the floor-managers and
salespeople patiently displayed their wares and answered
us in the politest newspaper Latin. Somewhere, on some
top floor, the Holy Spirit occupied His revolving chair-
manship, on the lookout for safe investments. In every
president's office of every building, God the Father
leaned back in a leather chair, His ankles crossed on the
desk, while in the room with the bare lightbulb His Son
added up figures for the final inventory.

But Aquinas' logic would quickly become oppressive,
even in his most interesting demonstrations. Three or
four pages of it and I would feel like one of those film ex-
traterrestrials, with balloon head and Giacometti body.
The parts of me that I had been suppressing would begin
to pound on their prison walls, and I would have to come
up for air, or rather, I'd have to come *out* of the air and
put my feet on solid earth, go for a walk or pull weeds in
the garden or feed my neighbor's horses over the fence
with some of the stale baguettes Elizabeth and I collect
from our local bakery: something, *any*thing, to escape
that deadly order.

After a week, though, my experience of Aquinas
turned around. I began to sense the man behind the logic.
Sometimes, as I sat with a bilingual *Summa* spread open
on the small cherrywood desk in my studio and gazed
out through the glass-paneled door into the branches of
the olive tree and beyond, my surroundings would dissolve into thirteenth-century Italy. The fantasy was so
vivid that I felt I was looking over Aquinas' right shoul-

der. I could see his shaven pate and ponderous body (he was a large man with an enormous appetite), the tilted dark wood of his writing desk in the monastery scriptorium, the parchment scroll and pot of blue-black ink and the long goose quill poised for a moment in his right hand as if about to take flight. And then, quickly across the page, stopping only to dip itself back into the ink pot, the pen would scratch forth line after elegant line of Lombardic script that spelled out the next elaborated detail in the life of the angels.

More and more I began to sense what was at issue with Aquinas and his predecessors. It had been staring me in the face through that sometimes impenetrable barrier of hyper-reasonable words. How could I not have understood that in writing about angels they were really writing about themselves? That the angel, whatever else it might be, is always an image of human possibility, because, as the German mystic Jakob Boehme said, "whatever the self describes, describes the self"?

Aquinas' reasoning about the angelic nature is the clearest instance of a mind enraptured by the act of contemplating perfection. As an exercise, I spent ten minutes one afternoon—a *long* ten minutes—trying to think about angels without using a single mental image. For a few moments I did feel a certain pleasure in this kind of thinking, the pleasure that a mathematician must feel in working out a complicated proof. I realized that the Angelic Doctor's description of angels is intellect contemplating intellect, like Saul Steinberg's drawing of a hand drawing itself. Except that the contemplation is penetrated with an unstated but constant sense of poignancy. This is a subtle emotion, and an odd one. The prose itself gives barely a hint of any emotion at all. But the emotion is there, just beneath the surface of the words. It is nothing so passionate as a longing for what the angels have, and not precisely envy or admiration of them. The emotion is what you might feel if you looked in the mirror and saw a face that was an almost unrecognizably beautiful version of your own face. In this sense, Aquinas is intellect thinking beyond intellect, as if a two-dimensional hand were drawing itself in three dimensions.

The angel of Aquinas is pure intelligence, freed of any limits imposed by its union with matter. Since the angel has no body, he is neither "he" nor "she"; since he has no sexual incompleteness to overcome, he is whole in a way that a human either-male-or-female can never be. Not only is he not divided into sexes, he is not divided at all; he is whole in all possible ways. He is the ideal intellectual, the thinker's thinker, the created being who most completely understands the truth. There is nothing more sublime in the whole universe, according to Aquinas, and nothing we can more rightly aspire to. "The ultimate human felicity is found in the operation of the intellect, since no desire carries us to such heights as the desire to understand the truth. Indeed, all our desires for pleasure or for other things can be satisfied, but the desire to understand does not rest until it reaches God."

As opposed to the human intellect, however, the angel has no need to observe the world, no need to acquire knowledge from material things; he is able to dispense with the clumsy mechanism of reasoning, since he has direct understanding of the way things are. He knows the truth intuitively, entirely, and within himself. In the act of intuiting one truth, he instantaneously grasps all its manifold consequences. The Eureka moment, Newton's apple or Kekulé's snakes, the breath-stopping inspiration, the dazzle of insight that sees heaven in a wild flower—these are the normal modes of his intelligence. Nor does he communicate by a means so gross as speech; his communication is immediate and complete; for him, empathy and telepathy are synonymous. His mind is to the human mind what dancing is to slogging through mud.

The most poignant aspect of Aquinas' contemplation of angels is his sense of their beatitude. Here, we are in a thought-world that it is difficult for non-Christians, and even for many contemporary Christians, not to be appalled by, a world that for most of us has mercifully been left behind. To a Christian of the second or of the eighteenth century, human life hovers between salvation and damnation, and until the Last Judgment, however loving and good you have been, you can never be certain, given the inherited corruption of the human soul, that God hasn't condemned you to eternal torment. But the bliss that an angel feels is inseparable from his absolute safety, his permanent state of grace. According to Christian theology, at the first moment of creation both the good and the bad angels made a single decision, once and for all time. "Each angel obtained bliss instantly,"

Aquinas wrote, "as a result of just one meritorious act." Afterward, there was no possibility of sin for them—they were incapable of it by definition—just as for Satan and the rest of his crew there was no possibility that God would ever forgive their one act of disobedience. "The nature of the angels is such that it was created to attain beatitude or to fall from it at the first choice, irrevocably."

I concluded this section of Chapter Two with a long contemplation of Aquinas contemplating the world of angels. He is sitting in his study in a monastery outside Naples. (I gave him the set of arched and latticed windows from Dürer's *St. Jerome*, with cushions and oversized books on the bench beneath, and the sill on which a user-friendly skull stares, suffused with late-morning light.) The world of angels is fully present to his mind, not as imagined form but as intelligible truth. No choirs, as in Dante, no brilliant concentric circles, no white multifoliate rose. Instead, an inconceivably joyful society of disembodied beings more numerous than the stars, hierarchically ranked by the quality of their intelligence, all participating in the beatific vision to the fullness of their vast and vaster capacities. He understands, down to the slightest detail, what the angelic mind must be like, but as he penetrates further and tries to enter that mind, he contemplates an intelligence that he with his powerful human intellect can barely fathom. Billions upon billions of these lovely, love-informed minds direct the planets and guide the affairs of men, all in many-layered harmony with one another, all in supernal bliss. They shine through his understanding like the light that shines through his study window. All of them know the ultimate truth. All of them are forever saved. A sigh, which he is too absorbed to notice, slowly swells the cavity of his massive chest, breathes itself out through his nostrils, and dissipates into the colorless, featureless, all-receiving air.

6

Near the end of his life, Thomas Aquinas, prolific writer, preeminent theologian, Doctor of the Church, advisor to kings and popes, had an experience of the Unthinkable, the God beyond God. It overwhelmed him. As a consequence, he never wrote another word. Silence was apparently a more eloquent response, and then death. He said only one thing about what had happened: "After seeing this, all my philosophy seems to me like a wisp of straw."

7

The classic angel literature, from Philo to Aquinas, was fascinating in many ways. But for all its fascination, I found very little in it that seemed to proceed from actual insight: little, in other words, that had not been written from a purely intellectual standpoint, rather than from a direct (and thus angelic) intuition of spiritual truth.

I did, however, come across a few exceptions. I included in Chapter Two a mini-anthology of passages that had caused a resonance in me, the kind that a poem can cause when it breathes down your spinal column like a kid blowing into an empty soda bottle and you feel, "Ah, this poet has *seen* something."

Avicenna, for instance, that learned Bukharan whore-master, in a startling insight that shuffles the traditional hierarchy like a deck of cards, wrote, "Each of the angels exists in a separate heaven, different from that of all the other angels. For because angels do not have bodies, they do not occupy space, nor is any of these heavens a physical place that can contain a physical being. That is why each angel exists in the whole of its heaven." Or this burst of delighted recognition from John of the Cross: "Even the wisest angel is perpetually surprised by God." Or from the eighteenth-century Swedish scientist and clairvoyant Emanuel Swedenborg: "The more angels, the more room." (This third example is all the more impressive since Swedenborg's usual accounts of angels as exemplary bourgeois churchgoers make heaven seem like the most boring city in the world.) Or two passages from Meister Eckhart, deepest and cheerfulest of Christian mystics, who lived a generation later than Aquinas: "A single spark that fell from even the lowest-ranking angel would be enough to light up the earth with bliss." And: "Every angel exists in every other angel as completely as he exists in himself. And every angel, with all his bliss, fully exists in me, as does God Himself, though I don't know it."

The longest example of what I thought was genuine perception came from my friend Saul's favorite author, the medieval Jewish theologian Benjamin ibn Ezra (1037–1108), a rabbi and physician who lived in Cordova under the Moorish caliphs. He is on occasion the least abstract of theologians. This may be because he is temperamentally less a philosopher than a teacher of a particularly sweet and visual form of Jewish devotion, and isn't so much interested in defining reality as in expanding it.

Ibn Ezra is primarily known for two of his Hebrew works: *The Way of the Devout*, a manual for the contemplative practice of opening the heart (it remained popular among the Sephardim for seven hundred years), and *The Inner Garden*, an efflorescent mystical commentary on the Song of Songs. During the last year of his life, blind, honored, and grieving over the death of his eldest son, he wrote a short treatise in Arabic, entitled *Before the Beginning*, on the creation and character of the angels. This work remained in manuscript until 1626, when it was printed in Livorno, and its first English translation, by my friend Thomas C. Applebaum, didn't appear until 1982. Most of the book captured my interest only tangentially; by the time I came to it, I was up to my eyeballs in angelology, having just finished writing my fifteen pages on Pseudo-Dionysius. Besides, this kind of deductive reasoning from Biblical texts was done with greater brilliance and rigor by Aquinas a century and a half later. But there was one passage toward the end of the treatise—ibn Ezra's exegesis of Genesis 18—that seemed real to me as the most brilliant pyrotechnics of the intellect could not. This man was somehow speaking about his own experience; he had seen something, if not in the angelic mind, then in the human soul. (I quoted a more extensive excerpt in *Against Angels*, along with Tom Applebaum's insightful notes, which I omit here.)

> We do not know much about angels [this after a hundred-fifty-odd pages of elaborate speculation!] nor do we know

it with certainty, as we can with perfect certainty know the presence of God (may He be exalted). For while that knowledge is of the intellect, this knowledge is of the heart. But Holy Scripture tells us the stories of our ancestors who have seen angels, and in their seeing we too, after a fashion, can see. Among those who were blessed with an angelic visitation, none was more blessed than our father Abraham. . . .

Abraham, we are told, had settled in Hebron, by the great oaks of Mamre. *And as he sat before his tent in the* Gen. 18:1f. *heat of the day, he looked up and, behold, there were three men standing near him.* Now Holy Scripture does not say, *behold, there were three angels standing near him.* Why? Because the angels looked exactly like men. They did not have wings. They did not have the kind of luminous aura which, people say, is ascribed to them in the paintings of the Nazarenes. They did not stand, move, or speak in any manner that was not fully human. Perhaps they were not beautiful; *probably* they were not, since their intention was to appear as ordinary human beings. Perhaps one of them was short and stout; another was too thin, his eyes were too close together, he spoke with a lisp; the third one stooped, he had a sparse red beard, a bald spot on his head, and a pimple on his nose. When Abraham looked at them, he saw three men, no more and no less. They sounded like men, they smelled like men, if he had touched them he would have touched the warmth of human flesh. And when they had rested and washed their dusty feet with the water that Abraham had brought, and when they were served human food by their so courteous host, they ate the bread and yogurt and roast veal just as men would eat them, with a pleasure sharpened by physical hunger, conversing and laughing in good fellowship under the oak tree, as Abraham stood there listening to them and watching them with a full heart.

What does this teach us? If angels can take on bodies and appear in ordinary human form, no different from you or me, even to the perception of a man as surpassingly holy as our father Abraham (blessed be his memory), then anyone we meet may in fact be an angel. Thus benevolence, which according to reason and the law of nature is of such high value in the everyday affairs of humans, seems all the more necessary, since we must always realize that even the most ill-favored stranger is perhaps a being of light who has stepped for a while into this mortal body

Deut. 15:10 of flesh and blood. Therefore it is said, *Give generously to the stranger, and the Lord your God will bless you in everything you do.* And it is not only strangers who deserve our heartfelt welcome and acceptance. How can we be certain but that one of our neighbors or next of kin, one of our servants or tradespeople—the maid scrubbing our kitchen floor or the blacksmith shoeing our horse or the beggar lying in squalor outside the city gate—is an angel who for some hidden purpose has been commissioned to dwell among us, not for a few hours but for many years, for a whole human lifetime perhaps? Thus it is incumbent upon us to treat each of our fellow human beings with the utmost respect, as if he might be the temporary dwelling place of one of God's angels (blessed be their holy names). . . .

Abraham stood under the oak tree ministering to his guests as they ate, while Sarah, having hurried to bake bread and prepare the noonday meal, sat listening to their conversation and looking out at them from the entrance to the tent. Of the effect the angelic visitors had on Abraham, who was ninety-nine years old, and on Sarah, who was eighty-nine, we are told very little. In fact, we are told only one thing: that exactly nine months after the visit, Sarah gave birth to their beloved child, their darling, Isaac.

What had happened? It was not only that a divine promise had been given to them. The promise in itself was insufficient. Though God (may He be exalted) made it in potentiality, the promise needed human agents to manifest it in actuality. God would not immaterially fertilize a human womb, as the Nazarenes dream that He did with their Mary, alas. That would be to dishonor the act of love, as if (God forbid) sexual pleasure were a sin, or as if the love between a man and a woman were not holy enough to result in the holiest of offspring.

Sarah did not at first believe the promise, and for good reason. She laughed to herself at its absurdity. How could a very old man, whose sexual organ had for many decades been incapable of standing upright, come in to his very old wife and plant his seed in her, who *had long ceased to have* periods *after the manner of women*? The actualization of the promise needed something more than the promise itself. It needed the presence of the angels.

Gen. 18:11

Angels—as I have previously deduced from the properties necessarily inhering in the angelic essence—notice only briefly those human qualities that are accidental or merely personal. What they see and address in a human being is the image of God in his soul. They do not look at the eyes, but into the eyes and (as it were) directly through them. They do not sense the person, but the person behind the person. They do not speak to Jacob or Joseph, Esther or Rebecca, but to Adam, to Eve.

That is why—although you and I in our ignorance may not be able to recognize an angel when he addresses us

through a human form—those with pure hearts, as our
father Abraham's and our mother Sarah's were, surely
became aware that they were being most deeply seen and
most deeply loved by the three visitors. As the hours
passed and the guests ate and conversed, Abraham and
Sarah, to their great astonishment, felt younger and
younger. They felt the life blood waking up inside their
veins. They felt that anything was possible, that even the
fulfillment of the promise, as laughable as it had seemed,
was an event that might, that would, come to pass. And
after the angels had left them, giving cordial thanks for
the food and the hospitality, Abraham turned to Sarah
with love in his eyes and with an all-compelling physical
desire in his loins. He saw her, as he himself had been seen,
far beneath her outward bodily form. Though she was an
old woman with wrinkled skin, she appeared to him
as she had appeared when he first loved her. And when
Sarah looked at Abraham, she saw the essential man, and
herself mirrored in beauty in his eyes.

Inside the tent, naked, as the cool of the evening
approached, Abraham stood erect in all the glory of his

Psalm 19:5

manhood, *as vigorous as a bridegroom, and rejoicing like an
athlete as he runs a race.* And Sarah, whose sexual organ,
withered with age, had fallen into itself like a dead flower,

Gen. 18:12

found herself *moist with pleasure* in the embraces of her
masterful lover, filled with his seed and overbrimming
with joy.

8

The transition from Chapter One to Chapter Two of
Against Angels was fairly easy because, though it was from

the shallow to the thoughtful, the discussion still centered on images within the Jewish and Christian traditions. My third chapter, "Every Angel Is Terrifying," ventures into a more uncharted realm.

Contemporary "accounts" describe angels, without exception, as comforting: people who say they have had angelic visitations feel joyous, affirmed, light-filled, love-filled, etc. Why then is the human response in the Bible so often one of dread? What do the angels need to assuage by saying, as if to a child, "Do not fear"? Why, at the voice of the angel, does the prophet Daniel collapse onto the ground, "trembling upon my knees and upon the palms of my hands"? Why would anyone be afraid of a being who is pure light and love, or be shaken by a deeper level of fulfillment breaking through into our own reality?

This question has been treated by the German scholar Rudolf Otto in his *The Idea of the Holy*, which I discussed at some length. And it is true that at one level, the level of the unprepared soul, fear is indeed the mark of a genuine encounter with the divine, the *mysterium tremendum*, which demands that you take off your shoes, "for this is holy ground," and then demands that you take off your feet. That sense of the awesome appearing as the awful is what I found lacking in all the contemporary accounts, which make even Luke's heavily mythologized story of the shepherds abiding in the fields seem genuine by contrast: "And, lo, the angel of the Lord came upon them, and the glory of the Lord shone round about them: and they were sore afraid."

But fear is also the mark of the mind's unripeness.

Where there is no clinging, there is no fear. The most helpful image of such encounters is the primary image in *The Tibetan Book of the Dead*. According to this text, in the moments just after death each of us sees nothing but the clear light of our original nature. If we are mature enough (through spiritual practice or through natural capacity), we immediately merge into that clear light. If, on the other hand, we still cling to our assorted delusions and cravings, we will experience this light as unbearably painful, just as someone coming from a dark room into the sunlight will have to shield his eyes, and we will be drawn back to the great wheel of suffering, to softer, bearable lights and other, less authentic, modes of existence.

I took the chapter title from Rainer Maria Rilke's *Duino Elegies*, the profound, thrilling masterpiece that is widely acknowledged to be the greatest poem of the twentieth century. Much of this chapter was a discussion of Rilke's angels. I had studied Rilke's poetry in graduate school, but I hadn't spent much time with it since then. Anyone writing about angels, though, needs to pay serious attention to Rilke, because his is the subtlest intelligence in which the figure of the angel has been reflected. This statement may sound surprising, given the formidable intellects of Aquinas and other medieval theologians. But their minds were molded into a certain standardized shape by the theological dogmas that they believed. And because they had to accept the Bible's accounts as literal truth, they were all starting from, at best, second-hand information, if information it was. Besides, their angels were all thought-angels. Rilke didn't think with his mind. He had a more direct line to reality. He was a true poet, and thought with his whole body.

Rilke wrote about angels all his life. His earlier angels are lovely: supple-meaninged and light-winged as even the most graceful Leonardo or Raphael angel can't be, since, rather than in the gravitas of paint, these angels are embodied in the invisible element of words. The most charming of the early angels is the speaker in a poem called "Annunciation" (it is Gabriel, of course, though Rilke doesn't name him). Standing in front of Mary in the little room that has suddenly overflowed with his presence, the angel is so enchanted by her ripening beauty that he forgets the message he was sent to announce.

But even in these poems there are hints of the later Rilkean angel. The strongest hint appears in "The Angel," from *New Poems*. Like Jacob's angel, the figure here is the embodiment of challenge, who "with tilted brow dismisses / anything that circumscribes or binds." The poem ends with an image of life-transforming and self-shattering confrontation. If you were to give yourself over to this angel, Rilke tells the reader, someday, some night, the angel's light hands

> would come more fiercely to interrogate you,
> and rush to seize you blazing like a star,
> and bend you as if trying to create you,
> and break you open, out of who you are.

But it is in the *Duino Elegies* that the image of the angel becomes truly awe-inspiring. Once you begin to live inside the poem, as I did for a long time while I was working on this chapter, Rilke's angels seem more and more stunningly authentic. You have the sense that they are not a mere literary symbol, that whatever reality it is that sings its dark music through the classical German dactyls of the verse, it is something that Rilke has penetrated to, not invented. And in fact there is a story behind the poem.

Rilke had always been a prolific poet. But the completion of his famous novel, *The Notebooks of Malte Laurids Brigge*, in Paris in 1910, had left him shattered and hollow. The book had immersed his imagination in the most difficult realities that he associated with big-city life: loneliness, poverty, alienation, illness, paranoia, despair. His hero's, and his own, sense of ego boundaries grew so paper-thin that, in a weird variation of the Golden Rule, he found himself involuntarily taking on the spiritual devastation of his neighbors, of the whole city. By the time he had finished, he was exhausted. He wandered around Europe for two years, confused, more restless and unhappy than usual, terminally stuck. He wrote a few poems, but they were nothing much. He thought of giving up poetry, of enrolling in medical school. Nothing seemed to make sense.

Then, in the winter of 1912, he received an invitation from a wealthy friend, Princess Marie von Thurn und Taxis-Hohenlohe, to spend a few months at one of her homes, Duino Castle on the Adriatic Sea. She stayed for a while, with a large party of family, guests, and servants, then left him there alone.

One morning in late January—the story comes to us from Rilke through the princess's memoir of him—he received a troublesome business letter, which he had to take care of right away. Outside, a violent north wind blew, though the sun was shining. He climbed down to the bastions, which, jutting out to the east and west, were connected to the foot of the castle by a narrow pathway along cliffs that dropped off two hundred feet into the sea. He walked back and forth, absorbed in the problem of how to answer the letter. Then, all at once, he stopped. From the raging wind, what seemed to him an inhuman voice, the voice of an angel, was calling: *"Who, if I cried out, would hear me among the angels' hierarchies?"* He took out the notebook that he always carried with him and wrote down these words, and a few lines that followed, as if he were taking dictation. Then he climbed back up to his room, set his notebook aside, and (I love this detail) with true Germanic thoroughness, orderly even in the face of cosmic inspiration, first answered the business letter and then continued the poem. By the evening, the whole of "The First Duino Elegy" had been written.

What kind of event was this? That Rilke actually heard the voice of a non-physical intelligence coming from the storm is possible. That the voice was Rilke's own is certain: it speaks with the poet's "I," in the gorgeous classical rhythms of Rilkean verse. But there is no either/or here. In such intensities of experience, the very idea of outside or inside is irrelevant; psychic resonance spreads through the whole universe of matter; what is given by God is given by the innermost self. Whatever the voice was, angel and self, it came from the depths of life, and it came with an incontrovertible sense of mission. Rilke knew that this poem was to be his own justification.

The angel of the *Duino Elegies* is a figure of total fulfillment, total innerness. In a letter of 1915 Rilke talks about his experience of the Spanish landscape as his own personal analogy to angelic perception: "There the external Thing itself—tower, mountain, bridge—already possessed the extraordinary, unsurpassable intensity of those inner equivalents through which one might have wished to represent it. Everywhere appearance and vision merged, as it were, in the object; in each one of them a whole world was revealed, as though an angel who encompassed all space were blind and gazing into himself. This, a world seen no longer from the human point of view, but inside the angel, is perhaps my real task."

"The First Elegy" begins with the voice that Rilke heard in the wind, his own uncried cry of longing and intimation:

> Who, if I cried out, would hear me among the angels'
> hierarchies? and even if one of them pressed me
> suddenly against his heart: I would be consumed
> in that overwhelming existence. For beauty is nothing
> but the beginning of terror, which we still are just able to
>   endure,
> and we are so awed because it serenely disdains
> to annihilate us. Every angel is terrifying.

Commenting on this passage in a letter written thirteen years later, Rilke describes the angel in greater detail:

> The "angel" of the Elegies has nothing to do with the
> angel of the Christian heaven (it has more in common
> with the angel figures of Islam). The angel of the Elegies

is that creature in whom the transformation of the visible into the invisible, which we are accomplishing, already appears in its completion. For the angel of the Elegies all the towers and palaces of the past are existent because they have long been invisible, and the still-standing towers and bridges of our reality are already invisible, although still (for us) physically lasting. The angel of the Elegies is that being who guarantees the recognition in the invisible of a higher order of reality.—Therefore "terrifying" for us, because we, its lovers and transformers, still cling to the visible.—All the worlds in the universe are plunging into the invisible as into their next-deeper reality; a few stars intensify immediately and pass away in the infinite consciousness of the angels —, others are entrusted to beings who slowly and laboriously transform them, in whose terrors and delights they attain their next invisible realization. We, let it be emphasized once more, we, in the sense of the Elegies, are these transformers of the earth, our whole existence, the flights and plunges of our love, everything, qualifies us for this task (beside which there is, essentially, no other).

Death is the side of life that is turned away from us and not illuminated. We must try to achieve the greatest possible consciousness of our existence, which is at home in both these unlimited realms, and inexhaustibly nourished by both. The true form of life extends through both regions, the blood of the mightiest circulation pulses through both: there is neither a this-world nor an other-world, but only the great unity, in which the angels, those beings who surpass us, are at home.

The primary description of angels in the Elegies—and by far the most beautiful description of them in all litera-

ture—appears at the beginning of "The Second Elegy."
(The reference is to the apocryphal Book of Tobit, in
which the archangel Raphael, appearing in human form,
offers himself as a guide to the young man Tobias on an
important journey.)

Every angel is terrifying. And yet, alas,
I invoke you, almost deadly birds of the soul,
knowing about you. Where are the days of Tobias,
when one of you, veiling his radiance, stood at the front
    door,
slightly disguised for the journey, no longer appalling;
(a young man like the one who curiously peeked through
    the window).
But if the archangel now, perilous, from behind the stars
took even one step down toward us: our own heart,
    beating
higher and higher, would beat us to death. Who *are* you?

Early successes, Creation's pampered favorites,
mountain-ranges, peaks growing red in the dawn
of all Beginning,—pollen of the flowering godhead,
joints of pure light, corridors, stairways, thrones,
space formed from essence, shields made of ecstasy, storms
of emotion whirled into rapture, and suddenly, alone,
mirrors: which scoop up the beauty that has streamed from
    their face
and gather it back, into themselves, entire.

Here the angel becomes pure metaphor, protean, lucid, breathless. I wrote several pages about these glorious
lines, with their mixture of love and dread and almost
unbearable longing. Ultimately, though, there is not

much one can say about such magnificence. One can only point and admire.

But I knew something of what Rilke was writing about.

9

In February 1976 (eleven months before my first spiritual opening), I began a hundred-day solitary retreat, the third such retreat that I felt compelled to do in those years when I was a very young Zen student, unripe, stubborn, and famished for the real.

This particular retreat took place in a tepee on some land owned by a friend of mine, four hours north of San Francisco. My schedule, which had been handed down in a tradition that was more than a thousand years old, was a rigorous one: twenty hours of meditation a day, in fifty-minute periods of sitting followed by ten minutes of circular walking, with four hours of sleep a night in two two-hour shifts.

A week before I left, Sumi-sahn gave me a warning and a few survival instructions. "These hundred-day trainings are not so easy," he said. "You will either die, go insane, or get enlightened. Tell me: are you a lion or a sheep?"

"A lion," I said, though at that moment I felt more nervous than carnivorous.

"You must not forget," Sumi-sahn continued, "that everything you see or hear is your own mind. You may meet buddhas; you may meet demons. Don't pay special attention to them. Just let them come and go. Remember that when the truth appears, it is beyond anything you can perceive."

And to emphasize the delusiveness of all visions, he told me about a nineteenth-century Korean monk who did a hundred-day retreat in a hut on his monastery's land. Two-thirds of the way through the retreat, the monk had a vision of Amitabha, the Buddha of Infinite Light, who materialized before him, complete with a pulsating multicolor aura and a face of such profound compassion that the monk burst into tears of joy. Amitabha leaned over to him and with great love in his voice said, "You are very close to enlightenment now, dear child. There is only one small step left." The monk bowed to the ground and said, "Yes, Lord. Tell me. I'll do anything you say." Amitabha said, "The last step, dear child, is to cut off your penis." Which the monk proceeded to do. His scream was heard even in the village, a mile away.

I arrived at the retreat site on a Friday afternoon, February twenty-first. My friend Trumbull, the one who owned the land, drove me to a spot on a dirt road three miles away from the tepee, helped me backpack my supplies through the woods, and left me there with a promise to come get me on the first of June. It was a cold, drizzly day; the ground had turned to thick mud. I spent a couple of hours digging a trench around the tepee to keep the rain out, pulling the canvas up to the top of its poles, and stuffing the torn places with some plastic garbage bags I'd happened to bring along. Then, at five the next morning, I began to settle into the rhythms of meditation, reeling with fatigue during the first few weeks, and colder in my motionlessness than I ever dreamt I *could* be, even with five layers of padding (insulated undershirt, woolen shirt, heavy sweater, down vest, down coat). For my nightly vigils, I also wrapped myself from head to toe in my sleeping bag, and would have looked—had there been any observers—like some huge, blue, shivering caterpillar.

I didn't have any human visitors, except for a few moments in early April, when, as I was circumambulating the tepee during a period of walking meditation, three bare-chested hikers walked by—two young men and a young woman with bare (and shapely!) breasts, looking as surprised by the apparition of me as I was by them. There were, of course, animal visitors: a pair of rabbits who would drop by for an enthusiastic game of rabbit-tag every day at sunrise; hundreds of small birds; hawks; deer; a large unseen creature who once lumbered past the tepee at two A.M., snorting. And mice. During the first couple of months I used to hear them continually as I meditated, digging inside the rain-trench for hours, making a small steady noise like fingernails across a board. Every so often, one of them would pop in beneath the canvas and sniff its way toward the bottles of granola and dried fruit that I kept by my little makeshift altar, or trot up to me and sit back on its haunches, paws together as if in prayer, sometimes so close that I could see the small breath-clouds puffing from its nostrils. One night I forgot to screw the lid back on the honey jar, and I woke up to find one of my mice drowned in six inches of honey.

Anyone who has undergone the experience of spiritual transformation knows how difficult it can be. It is like cleaning the heart with a piece of steel wool. Or, as I later came to think, like that terrace in Dante's *Purgatorio* where the spirits who have stopped for a while to talk, dive back into the purifying, excruciating flames. They choose to return to their pain, to stand again in the pale blue archways of primal grief or rage where the heat is most intense, because their most ardent wish is to be burned free of all self-absorption, and ultimately to disappear, into God's love. (The fire is consciousness.)

I didn't die or go insane—or get enlightened, then—but I did spend many days in very peculiar mental realms. The grueling schedule was designed partly to weaken resistance and blur all personal boundaries, physical and mental. And the border between realities did in fact become very fluid. It would often fluctuate and disappear. I couldn't always tell the difference between inner and outer or recognize when some unconscious agenda had spilled out onto the physical landscape. There were whole weeks during which my subterranean giants broke loose and I felt overwhelmed by vast dramas of repressed energies forcing their way through my consciousness like human volcanoes. There were days when, during each period of walking meditation, obsessed with the man on the Quaker Oats box—his smiling face seemed to me the symbol of America at its best, a home-grown bodhisattva, the cheerful embodiment of health and wisdom that I myself would be when things settled down in my life and my path became easy, or easier—I would circle the tepee hugging the cereal box (granola with raisins) to my chest and weeping uncontrollably. Throughout all of this, my only job was to sit there amid the psychological debris stirred up by the meditation like a roto-rooter, not getting caught in it or judging it, but letting things appear and disappear as they wished.

On the eighty-second day I had a vision. It took place in one of those in-between realms, as I was floating up into wakefulness from a relatively shallow sleep. It didn't feel like a dream. I was fully alert within my body. If it *was* a dream, it was an intensely vivid one, the kind that tugs at you for days, or pins you to the ground and will not let you go until you bless it.

I was standing in a bombed-out chapel. There was moss on the stone walls and long grass growing from cracks in the floor. All around, I could hear soprano voices chanting one single note, continuous, exquisite. As I drew closer to the wooden choir-stall, I saw five beings standing in it. I knew instantly that they weren't human. They had the faces of human children, but I knew that they were very ancient beings. They looked at me for a long time, without blinking, without a sign. The clear joy of their faces set my whole body throbbing, like a wound.

I had, as I said, been duly warned about visions. I knew that in the context of meditation—since the truth is beyond any separation between subject and object—all mental events, all things that a perceiving "I" might be capable of seeing, hearing, touching, or thinking, are in themselves distractions. All of them are neutral; they come and they go, with their attendant dramas. St. Teresa's ecstatic visions of God and a pain in the knees are of equal value: that is, of no particular value at all. They are just phenomena passing through your awareness.

Despite Sumi-sahn's warning, however, and despite my considerable caution, when I returned to the level of ordinary consciousness I felt homesick, more overwhelmingly homesick than I ever had before. So much so, that for the first and only time, I broke the retreat rules and went back to sleep for another hour, in the hope of once again standing in the presence of these radiant beings.

Whoever, *what*ever they were, my angels were devastating. It took me many years to integrate the experience and, as David later pointed out, *Against Angels* was a crucial part of that integration. By the spring of 1991, when I came to write Chapter Three, I was grateful for the devastation. It allowed me to write from the inside:

My point here is that we have to be ready to see everything. In the earlier stages of spiritual growth, the contemplation of fulfillment can be both magnetic and unbearable. Every angel is terrifying, because when we know what kind of fulfillment is possible in this life, the longing for it is magnified a thousand-fold, while our patience is still microscopic. Terrifying also because in the light of such fulfillment, our own unfulfillment becomes achingly clear.

At a further stage, though, if an angel should appear to someone who has found peace in his heart, they would face each other like two mirrors: bright, empty, each reflecting the other as infinite space. Only a spiritually mature person can stand there with no longing at all.

10

The Hasidic rabbi Menakhem Mendl of Rymanov once said to his teacher, Rabbi Elimelekh, "Every evening I behold the angel who rolls away the light before the darkness, and every morning I behold the angel who rolls away the darkness before the light."

"Yes," said Elimelekh, "when I was young I used to see that too. But I grew out of it, thank God."

11

I don't want to leave Rilke at Duino Castle with just one Elegy written. The sequel begs to be included, because it is one of the great human stories of obstruction and fulfillment. Here is the way I told it in Chapter Three:

"The Second Duino Elegy" was finished by the end of January 1912, along with the first stanza of the Tenth; the next year Rilke wrote three-quarters of the Sixth, and then the Third; and the Fourth in November 1915. But even when the momentum became sporadic and, after 1915, stopped altogether, with only four Elegies completed, the certainty of his task remained. It would be a long, excruciating lesson in patience.

When life occurs at this level of intensity, biography turns into myth. The myth here resembles that of Psyche and Eros. The god appears, then is gone; and the abandoned soul must spend seven years wandering in his traces. Finally, she arrives. The god enters, she is caught up in a fulfillment beyond her most extravagant hope. After this, a happy ending seems unnecessary.

Rilke moved from city to city during and after the War, holding to his certainty and his despair. When at last, at the Château de Muzot, he found the protected solitude he needed in order to plunge back into himself, he had no suspicion that another masterpiece would arise along with the rest of the Elegies, as their prelude and complement.

On February 2, 1922, he disappeared into the god. It was, he later wrote, "a hurricane in the spirit." For days and nights at a time he stayed in his upstairs room, pacing back and forth, "howling unbelievably vast commands and receiving signals from cosmic space and booming out to them my immense salvos of welcome." By February 5, he had written the twenty-six poems of the First Part of *The Sonnets to Orpheus*, "the most mysterious, the most enigmatic dictation I have ever endured and achieved; the whole first part was written down in a single breathless obedience." By February 9 he had finished the Elegies. By February 23, he was left with an additional Elegy that replaced the existing Fifth, the brilliant essay on God and sexuality called "The Young Workman's Letter," four shorter poems, and thirty-eight more Sonnets.

This is surely the most astonishing burst of inspiration in the history of literature. Inspiration, because it seems fundamentally different from what other modern poets, even the greatest ones, have known as the process of writing, with all its rawness and groping toward the genuine. There was nothing tentative here. These poems were born perfect; hardly a single word needed to be changed. The whole experience seems to have taken place at an archaic level of consciousness, where the poet is literally the god's or Muse's scribe. We are in the presence of something so intensely real that all our rational categories are useless. Who can respond to it without a shudder of awe? Rilke himself did. On February 9 he wrote to his publisher:

> My dear friend,
> late, and though I can barely manage to hold the pen,
> after several days of huge obedience in the spirit —, you
> must be told, today, right now, before I try to sleep:
>   I have climbed the mountain!
> At last! The Elegies are here, they exist....
>   So.
> Dear friend, now I can breathe again and, calmly, go on to
> something manageable. For this was larger than life—during these days and nights I have howled as I did that time
> in Duino—but, even after that struggle there, I didn't
> know that *such* a storm out of mind and heart could
> come over a person! That one has endured it! that one
> has endured.
>   Enough. They are here.
>   I went out into the cold moonlight and stroked the
> little tower of Muzot as if it were a large animal—the ancient walls that granted this to me.

In a sense, completing the Elegies meant leaving them behind. The tragic gives place to the rhapsodic; lament modulates into ecstatic appreciation of what can be achieved within our human limitations. "Praise this world to the angel," Rilke says in "The Ninth Elegy,"

not the unsayable one,
you can't impress *him* with glorious emotion; in the
   universe
where he feels more powerfully, you are a novice. So show
   him
something simple which, formed over generations,
lives as our own, near our hand and within our gaze.

And in *The Sonnets to Orpheus* he sings in utter acceptance of everything that is alive and earthly. Have there ever been poems so radiant with sensuous experience? The taste of an apple, a horse galloping across a meadow, a flower opening at dawn—all are so intensely present in their ephemeral beauty that outer turns into inner, sense into spirit. The wholeness, the transfigured body of these poems, is a return to the simplest human experiences of seeing and breathing, beyond thought: the immense, vibrant, dangerous world that every child lives in. Though it is transcendence, it leaves nothing behind. It is pure precisely because it goes nowhere.

Rilke's angels, those desolating perfections, are not central to the later Elegies, and in the Sonnets they don't appear at all. They were no longer necessary. Through his long years of patience he had exorcised them.

12

Hayim of Verona, Elizabeth's sixteenth-century kabbalist ancestor, was once asked by a disciple, "What do the blessed souls in heaven do all day?"

Hayim said, "They listen to the music of the angels."

The disciple said, "What is the music of the angels?"

Hayim said, "You can hear it only if you have no ears."

The disciple said, "Can *you* hear it, Master?"

Hayim said, "My ears hear it when they have no me."

13

My fourth and final chapter, "The Six Angel Pictures," is an attempt to map the terrain of the mind as it relates to the figure of the angel. The pictures are my adaptations of The Six Oxherding Pictures, a series by a Sung dynasty Zen Master named Tzu-te, in which the enlightened mind is portrayed as an ox that is found, tamed, ridden home, and finally disappears. Each picture indicates an increase in maturity of response compared with the preceding one, until we arrive at the last picture, which portrays the mind that has fully ripened and is fully at ease. (I have known two people—Sumi-sahn and David—whose minds had arrived at this place. While I was writing *Against Angels*, I thought that I myself had moved past the fourth picture, *Letting Go of the Angel*, into the fifth, *No Angel, No Self*. That's why I was disappointed when Gabriel first appeared.) Of course, one shouldn't take any categories too seriously: the map—even a pretty good one—is not the terrain.

Many readers were puzzled by this chapter, because even people who call themselves atheists live in a still-Christian culture and think in a still-Christian language, which looks upon a visit from an angel as a sign of grace, and considers prophets and saints to be as spiritually evolved as humans can be. So it was shocking for them to hear that visions—even the visions of the prophets—may ultimately be delusions or that "miracles" may be a sign of arrested development. (Some of the angriest letters I received were not in response to Yün-chü and the catering angels but to another Zen story I told, a deeply compassionate one about the ninth-century Zen Master Huang-po. Once, when he was on pilgrimage, he and a traveling companion came to a wide river. Without breaking stride, the other monk walked across the water and from the other shore beckoned to Huang-po to follow him. Huang-po said, "If I had known he was that kind of fellow, I would have broken his legs before we got to the river.") On the other hand, there were many readers, and even some angel-watchers, who found this the most helpful chapter in the book.

The Six Angel Pictures were elegantly reproduced on successive even-numbered pages, with accompanying texts facing them on the right. I had my publisher commission them from the Chinese-American artist Randall Lee, who did a superb job of suggesting classical Zen spareness in a contemporary Western style. As with the Oxherding Pictures, each of the Angel Pictures appears inside a brush-drawn ink circle.

I patterned the texts on the work of Tzu-te and of Kuo-an, another Sung dynasty Zen Master. Here I will omit the more discursive two- to three-page commentaries that follow each text, and include just a brief description of the pictures, along with their texts.

One: Longing for the Angel

The first picture is a drawing of a young man—one *presumes* it is a young man, although with his longish hair and loose-fitting shirt and pants he could as easily be a young woman—looking up into the sky, his brow shaded by his right hand. His face seems troubled, but there is something touchingly innocent about his posture. He apparently thinks that if he keeps waiting, eventually an angel will fly down and land on one of the branches of the large tree in the right foreground.

THE TEXT

This is the first stage of awakening. His longing for angels is really a longing for his true self. Steeped in delusion, he is not so deluded that he has stopped searching. Open to possibility, he still thinks freedom belongs to somebody else. He doesn't realize that when he becomes his own miracle, miracles will appear all around him. He is looking in the wrong direction. And in truth, at this stage any angel that flew down from heaven would only be a distraction. Give him a chair and a pair of binoculars. He'll be sitting here for a long time.

Two: Seeing the Angel

The second picture shows the young man kneeling in the left foreground. His knees and toes rest on the ink circle that frames the picture, so that he is in danger of sliding down its slope into one of the large rocks at the bottom. It is not clear whether his body is actually trembling, but obviously he is in shock. His eyes are large, his mouth wide open. Slightly farther back, toward the right, dressed in a long white robe and perched on a comfortable boulder, an angel is staring down at him. Its wings, partly unfurled, cover the upper third of the picture. The angel has quite a fierce expression on its face. Its eyes are close together. Its nose juts out like a hawk's beak.

THE TEXT

Yes, he has seen the angel. But the goal is just the beginning of the path. Since he still lives in the world of opposites, he is blown about by his versions and aversions like a feather in the wind. And what is he looking at, after all? The beauty that makes him shudder proceeds from his own eyes. How long will it be until he sees beyond the seen? How many ecstasies will he have to suffer before he finally comes to himself?

Three: Wrestling with the Angel

In the third picture, the young man is standing erect in the middle foreground, his arms extended stiffly, barely leaning to his right. His hands grip the angel's muscular shoulders. His right knee is wedged between its bent thighs. The angel, wingless, is wearing just a loincloth. It leans into the young man at a forty-five degree angle, like the hypotenuse of a triangle. Its limbs strain, its brow is contracted with effort. But there is the hint of a smile on its face.

THE TEXT

At last! He has come to grips with the essential point. There is neither heaven nor earth, holy nor unholy, just the mysterious other, bearing down on him with all its might. He has no choice now. It is not a question of victory or defeat. As long as he is grappled by an other, he is grappled by a self. And though he may not be aware of it in the midst of their sweaty embrace, the other wants nothing more than to be defeated.

Four: Letting Go of the Angel

Here the young man sits toward the right, on top of the second picture's comfortable boulder. He is facing the viewer, staring directly ahead into an undefinable distance. In his hands is a wooden flute. Apparently he has just been playing it and has paused, for a moment of meditation or reverie, before putting it to his lips again. The angel, naked, is tiptoeing off toward the left. It looks weary but content. One can't be sure, but it seems to be limping.

THE TEXT

The struggle is over; he no longer remembers who won. All thoughts of beauty and wisdom have flown out of his mind. Angels may come and he will bid them welcome; angels may go and he will wave goodbye. It doesn't matter. He has looked into the great mirror and seen all things in himself. Homage to the ant! Homage to the genius of the grass-blade! The light from before creation keeps pouring out of his heart.

Five: No Angel, No Self

The fifth picture is an empty circle. The brushstoke on this circle is more dramatic than on the circles around the other five pictures. It begins with a thick blotch like a snake's head, at about the 200-degree point, and then moves up and around to the right, thinning out past 90 degrees. By the time it rejoins itself, there is very little ink on the brush and only a few pale feathery lines tapering off into the emptiness of the white page.

THE TEXT

Both angel and young man have vanished: the angel because it has been completely integrated, the young man

because there is no one left to confront. He has stopped
looking outside or inside, and lets heaven take care of itself.
Like Yün-chü in front of his meditation hut, he has disappeared to all possible angels and disappeared to himself. He
has hung out a shingle on his front door that says *Vacancy:
come on in.* Serene in the midst of decay, he sits observing
the ten thousand things as they undergo changes.

Six: Entering the Marketplace with Angelic Hands

In the sixth picture, the young man has become middle-
aged, bearded, and smiling. His face is much fuller now. A
dark robe, draped casually around his shoulders, reveals a
hairy chest and a generous belly. The staff he holds in his
right hand has a large cloth bag tied to it. In his left hand he
holds a basket out to the viewer, invitingly. The trunk of a
plum tree curves up from the bottom left to the top left por-
tion of the circle. Its branches, extended over his head like a
canopy, are filled with blossoms.

THE TEXT

Vacation time! He has graduated from spiritual practice,
from obligations, from enlightenment. Now he is just hanging out, and the only thing he follows is his nose. His bag is
filled with gaudy knickknacks for the children: sutras, upanishads, bibles. Wherever he wanders, he is greeted by old
friends. He acts for the pure pleasure of it: in other words,
for the benefit of all beings. But all beings are already saved.
Open his picnic basket; take out the bread and wine. You
will find as much or as little as you need.

"**g**ood morning," Gabriel said as I walked down the brick path to my studio. It was Sunday, the day after our first meeting. I hadn't expected to see him again.

"Good morning to *you*," I said, amused. "Actually, it's two in the afternoon."

"Ah," he said, "yes, the sun." His nakedness was less of a distraction today. But how dazzlingly beautiful he was!

"Did you sleep well?" he said.

"Very well, thanks." Elizabeth and I had made love the night before. I knew she had sensed that there was something different about me. She kept looking up—or down—into my eyes with a flicker of intrigued recognition, but would then get swept back and reabsorbed into the intensity of her pleasure. We had slept in each other's arms until my snoring woke us at three and she turned away, burrowing into her pillows with a soft whimper. In the morning, it occurred to me that being open to the extraordinary is a way of embracing the ordinary more deeply.

"Let me bring over a couple of chairs," I said to Gabriel. "Do you want some lunch?"

"No, thank you, I'm fine. Yesterday's lunch was splendid, though. *Was* it yesterday?"

I chuckled. "You do seem like an old friend. Wait a minute. I'll be right back." As I walked toward the deck, Magellan, our neighbor's Maine Coon cat, who was sprawled out in the shade of the apple tree, lifted his head and greeted me with a voiceless meow. I wondered if he could see Gabriel, too.

I brought over the chairs and put them down between the olive and the pomegranate tree. Its bright orange-red flowers had just begun to thicken and swell into the darker red of the fruit.

"So," I said. "Why have you come back?"

"Because of you," he said, with a mischievous smile.

"Touché." And in truth I *had* been thinking a lot about our conversation, had even been composing a series of off-the-cuff mental revisions and addenda to *Against Angels*. Once my disappointment had faded, I could appreciate how far I'd come in my response to angels since my tepee retreat, nineteen years before. "I admit that I'd be happier *not* to see you," I said. "But I am very glad to see you."

"I'll take that as a compliment."

"Please," I said. "And if you wouldn't mind, now that you're here, I do have more questions."

"I'm at your service."

"Well, for one thing, there's your memory. I wonder about it. It seems so sporadic."

"Yes, that's true. I haven't entered your time enough times to quite get the hang of it. Just a few dozen, I think. It still seems very peculiar to me that this human mind preserves traces of the past and not of the future."

"Why peculiar? The future hasn't taken place yet."

"Oh?" he said. "But you see, I have visited realms where time is much more fluid or malleable than it is here. It runs backward, for example, from future to past, in worlds composed of what you would call anti-matter. Or it can run forward and backward like an alternating current. Or so that two sides of it, past and future, are visible at once. I have to keep reminding myself that in this body I can't remember the future. Then there are realities in which time has not three but ten modes, or a hundred."

"Like languages that have a hundred words for 'camel' or 'snow'?"

"Precisely," he said. "In those realms, they pay very close attention to time, and space has become vestigial. Of course, the realest reality is when time intensifies until there is only now."

"But what do you actually remember about this world of ours?"

"I've appeared mostly to children, or in ages that you

wouldn't have heard of. A few times to prophets, but I can't say with resounding success. They get so overwrought, these unstable types, who force their minds open by a *dérèglement de tous les sens*. Poor Daniel. My appearance pushed him over the edge, I'm afraid. Politics, predictions. He lost it completely."

"What about your visit to Mary? That's what you're most famous for, hereabouts."

"Mary? Mary who?"

"You know, the *Virgin* Mary."

"I'm sorry," he said, "but I can't seem to place the name."

"Mary of *Nazareth*."

"Oh, Miryam! Of course! A supremely beautiful soul, Miryam. I remember everything about her. But why do you call her 'Virgin'?"

"That's a long story."

"She was pregnant, you know."

"Yes, she was," I said. "Tell me about her."

He closed his eyes. The sweetest of smiles spread over his features.

"It was a small room," he said, looking at me again, "with a dirt floor and stone walls the color of peaches, a table, a chair, and a straw mattress. She was standing by the window. An extraordinarily lovely young girl, as graceful as a birch tree. I suddenly felt very young myself, very shy. My mouth opened in wonder, I could hear my heart beating, 'Shalom alayikh' came out in a whisper. 'So this is what it's like,' I thought, 'to be in love in a human body.'"

He paused. A minute went by.

"I had put on wings for the occasion, but the ceiling was too low for me to spread them in greeting. Besides, she was hardly aware of me. She registered my presence; smiled at me briefly; when I gave her the lily, she held out her right hand and accepted it with a little nod of thanks. But basically, she was absorbed, as if she were gazing into the clear depths of a crystal. She was deep within herself. There was such a richness of event happening in her, such a ripening into God's will, that my appearance was of the merest incidental nature. I knew I had come more for my sake than for hers."

"Had you ever seen a pregnant woman before?" I said.

"Well, of course, there was Sarah, Abraham's wife. But she seemed quite a bit older. And she was a . . . how can I put this kindly . . . ?"

"A shrew?"

"A difficult character," he said. "Her heart was frozen. It took a lot of radiance from all three of us to warm her up."

"Even afterward, though, she wasn't exactly sweetness and light."

"No? I'm sorry to hear that."

"But about Miryam . . ."

"She was so complete," he said, "and yet so wide open. Such purity of heart. So intensely female. I loved her very much. For a few moments, in my temporary flesh, I couldn't help imagining myself as the man who had come inside her. I had to blush. But she didn't notice."

"Can you remember how long you were in the room?"

"It seemed like eons. There were so many emotions. My heart was melting. I wanted to weep with pleasure. I wanted to kneel before her, but that would have bent the bottoms of my wings. It was as if, in paying homage to her, I was paying homage to all women. I was kneeling in spirit, before the fully human."

"Certainly, Jesus didn't pretend to be anything other than human."

"Jesus?" he said.

"Yeshu. Miryam's son."

"Oh. It was a boy?"

I nodded, slowly.

He closed his eyes. That sweet smile lit up his features. For five minutes or so, we were silent. Then he looked at me and said, "You have more questions."

"Yes," I said, "there *is* something else I've been wondering about. The various heavens you mentioned yesterday: Who lives in them and what are they like? And how is an archangel different from an angel, say, or a cherub? I've studied this, as you know, and the distinctions have always seemed pretty vague to me."

"Of course they're vague!" he said. "There's no taxonomy of the spirit. When you try to classify spiritual beings, all you're talking about is your own categories. It's not even that there are infinite variations within a species. Each individual *is* a species."

"So what does it mean to be an archangel?"

"Oh, just that we've been around longer than some of the others, and we've learned how to play more intricate games."

"How do you mean, 'longer'?"

"This is difficult to explain in human language. Of course, for beings who are, in your terms, beyond space and time, 'shorter' and 'longer' don't mean a lot. I'm not talking about duration so much as intensity."

"Oh?"

"And even in the universe of space," he said, "there is no absolutely higher or lower. So in one sense, the very name 'archangel' is a mistake. On the other hand, since this is a bipolar universe, there is always an 'other hand.'"

"Meaning that . . ."

"There is always an equally valid counter-truth. A truth as basic as two plus two equals four, for instance, isn't always true. Even in some of your arithmetics, two plus two equals five, or one. And with numbers too, as with angels, there are different kinds of infinity. Two beings may be equally infinite, but the capacity of one may be greater than the other's. Take the set of even numbers. Obviously, it has no upper limit, since after the largest even number I can name, you can always name a larger one."

"Yes . . ."

"Now take the set of whole numbers, both even and odd. It too is infinite."

"Okay . . ."

"But there are twice as many whole numbers as there are even numbers."

"True . . ."

"In other words, even though the set of whole numbers contains the set of even numbers, each set is infinite, and there is exactly the same number of numbers in each. So the whole is not necessarily greater than its parts."

"Interesting," I said. "But how does that apply to angels?"

"You don't see?"

"I'm afraid not."

"My dear fellow, it's really quite simple. Let's try from another direction."

"Okay. I'm sorry to be so dense, but math isn't my strong suit."

"That's all right. Just think of intensity in the human arts. It has nothing to do with largeness and everything to do with greatness."

"Yes, I understand," I said. "Vermeer, for example. You can't get more intensely intimate than that. His works are small, but he's as great an artist as Michelangelo, whereas a painter like Rubens or Titian, working on a much larger scale, is of the third or fourth order of greatness. Or in music, you could say that Bach equals Mozart equals Palestrina, whereas the intensity of a Purcell or a Rameau is something quite different."

"You see, don't you, that the two orders don't necessarily differ in quality."

"Yes," I said. "Purcell's a wonderful composer. His music is perfection itself."

"Still, they are different orders of intensity."

"So what you're saying is that an archangel is to an angel as Bach is to Purcell?"

"It's a very rough analogy."

"Ah. But that does make it clearer."

"When archangels play with angels," he said, "we are limited by their capacity, not solely by the rules of the game. It's like applied versus pure mathematics. Oh, sorry."

"That's quite all right."

"We can't play all-out. It's more like teaching."

"Rod Laver against the national junior champion?"

"Let's not take these analogies *too* seriously," he said. "It sounds silly, doesn't it?, to call Henry Purcell a junior champion. These teaching games are enjoyable in their own way, to be sure. But games with our peers are always the most thrilling. The fascination of the difficult."

"Do you ever play games with spirits who used to be human?"

"Very occasionally. Most of them are still in the transition period. It's difficult for humans to leave themselves behind."

"'Strange / to leave even one's own first name behind, like a broken toy,'" I quoted. Quoting great writers is a weakness of mine. It sometimes drives Elizabeth crazy.

"Exactly. Very good. Who wrote that?"

"Rilke. 'The First Duino Elegy': 'And being dead is hard work, / and full of retrieval before one can gradually feel / a trace of eternity.'"

"It *is* hard work for most of them," he said. "They tend to gravitate toward the lowest of the human heavens, where they feel more comfortable."

"Most people must be very surprised to be conscious after death, I would think."

"Yes, although children usually aren't. The distinction

between life and death is such a minor affair, but people on earth make a big to-do about it. They get so caught up in their negative thought-forms. Or in their positive ones, for that matter."

"How so?"

"Oh, the first heaven is filled with family reunions. Mother, Father, grandparents, dead children, all bathed in radiance, everybody hugging, everybody in tears. It's lovely, but it doesn't last."

"It doesn't?"

"The joy gets vitiated, of course. A hundred or a thousand years of celebration, and then what? Death doesn't solve any problems. Once the joy has worn thin, these spirits are once more faced with their personalities and their unfinished business. You have to understand that all the heavens are impermanent. Even the archangelic heaven. Even the heaven of the seraphim. Someday they will all disappear."

"But I thought you said that spirits are beyond time."

"That's true only in a manner of speaking. We live in such a different order of time that it's misleading to use the same word for it as you do. It is so vast and it moves with such glorious leisure that it seems not to exist. This time is a mode of eternity in the sense that we are present beyond past and future. But strictly speaking, only the *I Am* is eternal. Everything that has a beginning also has an end. Thank God."

"I'm confused now. What period of time are you talking about? A million years? A billion?"

"The lowest heavens last for about a kalpa."

"How do you define that?" I said.

"Imagine Mount Everest. Every thousand years an eagle flies past it, brushing it with its wing. A kalpa is the period it would take for the eagle to wear the mountain to the ground."

"A *very* long time."

"We estimate that *our* heaven lasts for about three billion kalpas."

"And then?"

"Then the momentum of our intelligence stops, and we drop down into one of the lower orders of being and have to start all over. But for the time being, we're enjoying ourselves."

"Wow," I said. "I'm stunned."

"I thought you might be," he said. "You still don't understand about joy and sorrow, and how blessed you humans are. It will all come clear, though, in the end. Would you like to take a field trip?"

"What do you mean?"

"The only way you'll understand the heavens is if you see some of them for yourself. I'd be glad to take you on a brief tour."

"Hmm," I said. "How long will I be gone? I have a dinner date with my wife, and there are a few things I have to finish up before I get showered and dressed."

"Less than five minutes of your time."

"You're sure now . . . You won't forget that you said 'minutes' and not 'centuries' . . ."

"Don't worry. Five minutes. I promise to bring you back."

"Well, okay. It's just that I still have things to learn here and now, and a pile of unfinished business."

"I understand. Do you trust me?"

I took a deep breath. "Yes, I do."

"Look at me then, and relax."

I took another deep breath and looked into his beautiful pale-blue eyes. Suddenly a curtain of brilliant white light was drawn across my vision. I could still see Gabriel's face at the center, the apple tree behind him and a corner of the studio to his right, but the rest of my view was blocked by the advancing curtain. Then there was only the brilliance. Everything else disappeared. I was aware that my heart had stopped, that I wasn't breathing, and I could see my skin turning gray. Yet I wasn't at all afraid. On the contrary, stepping outside my body in this way was exhilarating. I laughed out loud.

"This is wonderful," I said or thought. "This is just great. Helloooo, are you there?"

"Coming," Gabriel called. Then he appeared. He looked just as he had looked in his human form, but more translucent. "I needed to adjust the cord," he said, "so that your body won't be in shock when you return."

There was something extremely pleasant and yet peculiar about the way he was speaking. I knew that it wasn't in English or in any human language, and yet it wasn't quite telepathic either. Nor was it precisely a sound, though it had a certain mellifluous quality to it. The most accurate sensory analogy I can find is the experience of drinking a great vintage port—a 1977 Fonseca, for example. His speech entered me like that: a dark, rich, subtle, velvety liquid radiance that shimmered on my palate with the taste of a dozen fruits and left me feeling honored and elevated, as if I had been visited by an elder statesman of great wit and impeccable integrity.

For the first few . . . I suppose I should call them "minutes," I found the pleasure of his words distracting, and I had to will myself to pay attention to their meaning. But it was much easier to get adjusted to him here (if there was a *here*) than it had been on earth. The fascinating pull of his splendor was gone, since this realm seemed to be so light that there was no such thing as spiritual gravity. Soon I wasn't having any trouble at all.

"Where's the tunnel?" I said.

"Do you really want the tunnel?" Gabriel said. "That leads to the heaven of reunions. You won't learn anything there. I'd prefer to show you some other realms."

"Okay," I said. "You're the leader. I'll follow you."

He took my etheric hand.

Instantly we were somewhere else. I could no longer sense the body I had left on earth.

The first thing I saw (though "saw" isn't the right word) was an overwhelmingly brilliant light, which made the brilliance of the white curtain seem like the merest spark. The light was beautiful beyond words. It was loving beyond words. I was about to plunge straight into it, when I was yanked back.

"I promised to return you," Gabriel said. "Now you know. That single movement backward makes all of us possible."

I felt a twinge of . . . not regret or poignance, but happiness in a minor key, the assurance of an ultimate good that must, for a while, be postponed.

I looked around. There was only clear sky, with millions of flickering points.

"We are in the lowest heaven of the angels now," he said. "These minor angels have existed for only a few hundred kalpas. Let me introduce you to one of them."

An iridescent light shaped like a beach ball appeared on his right. He leaned toward it. "What did you say your name was?" he said. A sound somewhere between a whisper and a jingling of bells came from the ball. Gabriel turned to me and said, "This is Shiriel. Shiriel, Stephen."

"Hello," I said.

The ball glowed. Actually, it was as much a honk as a glow. It was the most hilarious form of greeting you can imagine. I burst into laughter. A dozen fragments of myself hurtled out into space. I immediately expanded, collected them, and willed myself back together. This process was equally funny. I had to concentrate hard, so as not to explode a second time.

"Don't stay out too long now," Gabriel said. Then he was gone.

What happened next was something that language can't possibly convey. I will try to translate it as well as I can into bodily, earthly terms. But these are just very rough approximations.

The iridescent ball darted toward me, then darted off; darted toward me, then darted off again and waited, quivering. I could sense that it was in a state of high exhilaration. Clearly, I was being invited to play, by a kind of superhumanly intelligent puppy. I had the urge to find a stick, for a game of fetch. This seemed so sweetly ridiculous that I almost burst apart again. After I did the nonphysical equivalent of biting my cheeks to keep myself from laughing, I felt my will somehow engaging with the angel's will. I darted off in pursuit of it.

I am describing this in the language of movement. But there was no movement. Nor was there music, though I will use the language of sounds. The game was happening in a realm of infinitesimally subtle distinctions, where the slightest hint of a thought created a major reality. It's as if what our human words can distinguish as feet and yards were happening in units of measurement appropriate to electrons.

Pursuing or running from Shiriel is one way of talking about the next phase. It was great fun at first, like romping in a meadow with a child. But it was also enormously demanding, and I soon found myself overextended and, as it were, out of breath. An equally valid way of describing the game is as a series of musical variations. The angel's darts and feints were ravishingly beautiful harmonic patterns, which I in some way was expected to respond to, to repeat or modify or elaborate. I found this bewildering, though at the same time I was fascinated. It was a thousandfold magnification of the experience, in my thirties, of falling in love with modal music, especially the music of Palestrina and Victoria: for weeks my ear was so unaccustomed to the new language that I couldn't distinguish composer from composer or even one particular Mass from the next. I now felt a similar, though much intensified, bafflement about these sounds. They were beyond my comprehension, yet so beautiful that I didn't know whether to laugh or cry or throw up my hands in despair. In the midst of all the exhilaration and rapture, I felt strained to the limits of my intelligence, as if I were being asked to play a difficult piano sonata after just learning the scales.

Then the music from the iridescent ball deepened and became so piercingly beautiful that I could barely endure it. During every moment that passed I felt that the depth and intricacy and simplicity and gorgeousness of it were too much for me, and at the same time, more than anything in the world, I wanted to hear the next sound, and the next. This phase of the game also is impossible to describe. I felt as if I were a mouse that was being toyed with by a supremely skillful and exuberant master-cat. Over and over I was caught and clamped between the rows of giant teeth, and I knew there was no way I could escape. Sometimes I would be set down on the ground and permitted the illusion of trying to escape. But after I scurried to the left or right, the cat would leap and clamp me, not with fury but with the most enchanting, murderous *joie de vivre*, in its teeth once more.

"All right, that's enough," Gabriel said, appearing just as I thought I was done for. The angel made a small, oboe-like bow to him and vanished.

Gabriel smiled at me. "Did you have fun?"

"Well," I said, catching my non-breath, "that's not quite the word I would use."

"Shall we move on to the next heaven? It's populated

by angels who are considerably riper in their intelligence."

"How much is 'considerably'?"

"If the intelligence of your playmate is one grain of rice on the first square of a chessboard," he said, "and if you double the grains for each successive square until you get to the last square, that will be the intelligence of the angels in this next heaven."

I did some multiplication. "Thank you," I said, "but I think I'll pass."

"Are you sure? Their capacity for love increases in proportion to their intelligence. They are very charming beings, I assure you. They'd enjoy playing with you."

"No, really, I'll take a rain check. I'm grateful to you, but that's about all the angel games I can handle right now."

"Oh. But I wanted to show you a few more angel heavens."

"How many different angel heavens *are* there?"

"Three hundred ninety."

"That's not counting the heaven of the archangels?"

"Or the heaven of the cherubim or seraphim."

"Maybe we should go in the *opposite* direction," I said. "Can we visit some of the lower heavens, where the human spirits are?"

"Of course, my dear. We'll do whatever you wish. We can go down and take a look at the third heaven, if you want, though I don't think you'll have a very good time there."

"Why the third heaven?"

"For the sake of your education."

"Fine."

He took my hand.

Instantly we were hovering above a large golden city that was surrounded by a wall made of what looked like massive emeralds. As we descended, I could see that the wall's foundations were encrusted with all sorts of precious stones: sapphires, diamonds, opals, lapis lazuli, rubies, topazes, amethysts, and other jewels that I couldn't identify. Each of the twelve gates in the wall was an enormous pearl, and the streets seemed to be pure gold, as transparent as glass.

"Let's wait here," Gabriel said after we touched down.

Hundreds of spirits were walking past us in orderly lines. They were going in one direction only, not in opposite streams, as you would expect in a crowded city. It was obvious that they were all headed to some destination and weren't just out for a stroll. They all wore smiles on their faces. Their spirit-bodies were shining and naked. None of them had genitals.

As I watched them pass, I began to feel that there was something peculiar about their faces. They resembled one another in a way that I couldn't put my finger on at first. Then I realized that, with their sleepy eyes and pale, slightly elongated lips and noses, they all looked like sheep.

We waited for a long time, but none of the spirits stopped to talk to us. Finally Gabriel intercepted one of them, a male, and herded him over to me.

"Hello," I said.

"Hello."

"Where are you headed?"

"Choir practice," he said.

"What are you practicing?"

"Look, I'd love to chat with you fellows, but I really have to go. See you around." And off he went.

"It's always like that here," Gabriel said. "These spirits are very happy now, after spending so much of their time on earth in doubt and confusion. Now everything seems clear, though their truth is only a dim reflection of the much larger truths of the fourth heaven. They need to have one way only, one truth only; it makes the *I Am* tolerable to them. They do everything together, they see everything the same way, they enter into a mutual goodness covenant and agree to become spiritual clones of one another. Not a very interesting heaven. But for them it is enough."

"Isn't this the heaven that Saint Paul visited? Paulus. Sha'ul of Tarsus."

"Ah, that troubled soul. Yes."

"The heaven he was 'caught up to'? Where he heard 'unspeakable words'?"

"Yes. From time to time, visiting preachers come here from more evolved heavens. But the words weren't unspeakable. John was able to speak them quite well: *God is love*. That was a painful lesson for Paul, because his mind was so filled with hatred. And for John too. They're still working at it. When they're not at choir practice."

I smiled. Smiling without a face is an interesting experience. You should try it sometime.

"Let's move on," Gabriel said. "How about going to some of the higher human heavens?"

"I'd like that," I said. "Could we visit William Blake?"

"Of course. He's a particular friend of mine. We can go to the hundred twenty-fourth heaven on our last stop."

"Thanks," I said. "I'd love to meet him."

Gabriel took my hand many times during the next untimable instants, and we visited many heavens: a heaven of fulfilled desires, where a spirit has only to imagine something for it to be true, and everything that seemed insuperably difficult in life (though after many millions of years in this heaven the excitement of it begins to pall) is accomplished with effortless ease: the unattainable woman falls in love with you, the unscalable cliff seems like a flight of stairs, every drive you hit goes three hundred yards down the center of the fairway, every poem you write is a masterpiece, you are beautiful, you are brilliant, you are adored, you speak French with a perfect accent; a heaven where—because the sole content of awareness is color, and because each spirit is like a man lying in a hot bath and with wonderment thinking only *yellow!* or *red!*—the meeting of two spirits is the merging of primary colors, and the more spirits come together, the more subtle and marvelous the palette of awareness becomes; a heaven of dried tears; a heaven of mutual vivid dreaming; a heaven where each spirit can choose to inhabit the idea of an animal body, the body of a favorite cat or dog or horse, for example, or of a lion, a whale, an eagle, and plunge into the immense world of delight that pure bodily experience is; a heaven of minor triads; a vast, mostly non-representational heaven, in a corner of which, on one of those lovely Italian spring mornings when nature's sap runs through the veins of the city, in a small Florentine piazza I saw a group of a dozen men clustered, arguing and laughing—Gabriel identified them as Bonaventure talking to Thomas Aquinas, Plato with the Yellow Emperor, the Baal Shem Tov, John Milton, an Ibo potter who died during the reign of Charlemagne, and Virgil (a handsome man in a double-breasted white suit)—and, in the center of the piazza, a bonfire which, as I approached, took on the gaunt, familiar, compound lineaments of Dante, angry even in heaven, burning with passionate intensity and savage indignation; a heaven of irreverence, where the most sacred truths are mocked or contravened in a cosmic vaudeville burlesque in which each spirit is both performer and audience, until the very concepts of sacred and profane vanish like the spangled girl behind the magician's curtain; a heaven of deflected childhoods; a heaven of parallel universes; a heaven of eroticism, where every flicker of desire becomes a tableau vivant that makes the Kama Sutra seem like a Sunday school primer, and every spirit is the pulsing clitoris at the center of a galaxy of concentric orgasms; a heaven of the ugly, where all the spirits look exactly as they did in their earthly life and the only thing that has changed is their own appreciating awareness (there is always one resident angel); a heaven of trees; a heaven of the Great Mother; a heaven of oblique returns.

Finally, after Gabriel took my hand once again, I found myself swimming through a cool rainbowy river of light inside what seemed to be a gigantic crystal. It was extremely invigorating. I plunged twenty feet below the surface, then leapt above it like a porpoise. Gabriel leapt with me.

After a while, we floated on our backs, side by side, and let the river carry us onward.

As we came to a certain bend, Gabriel said, "This is where we get out." We climbed onto the riverbank. I was dripping with rainbow-colored light.

When I looked up, I saw a short man sitting at a small round table. "There's Blake!" I said. "Over there!" I would have recognized him anywhere—his high forehead and compressed features, the chisel nose, the brilliant visionary eyes.

It was an outdoor café. Three men were sitting at a table not far from Blake's.

"Who are the others?" I asked.

"Mmm, let me see . . ." Gabriel said. "That one is Michelangelo, and the one with the beard is Isaiah, and then John Milton."

"But we saw Milton in the *other* heaven."

"We did. But this is Blake's Milton."

"Oh."

We walked over to the café. Michelangelo, Isaiah, and Milton each had a ruby-colored drink in front of him, in a long glass with a bright green straw sticking out of it. On the table was a platter of hors-d'oeuvres that Gabriel identified for me: cheese puffs, little frankfurters *en croûte*, caviar on wheat crackers, and pruninghook-shaped asparagus spears with a Chardonnay-and-mustard sauce. The three spirits were sipping and eating, and talking with great animation, though it was difficult to tell whether their language was Italian, Hebrew, or English, or some amalgam of the three. The tables seemed to be made of crystal, as did the chairs, the sidewalk, and everything else. Blake himself had a crystalline glow.

"Sit down, sir, sit down," he said to me, standing up and shaking my hand vigorously. "You are very welcome."

"It's a great honor to meet you, Mr. Blake," I said.

"I am glad to make *your* acquaintance," he said. "And you, Your Grace, how very kind of you to pay me a visit after so short an interval. Have you come to sit for your portrait again?"

"No, my dear," Gabriel said, "not this time. But I was honored by your last portrait. I showed it to Raphael, and he thought it an excellent likeness."

"Raphael the painter?"

"No, Raphael the archangel."

"Ah. Well, that is almost as good. But pray," he said, turning to me, "what brings you here, sir, and how may I be of service?"

"I'm visiting some of the heavens," I said. "I'm still alive—that is, I'll be returning to my body."

"I paid the heavens many a visit myself while I was still in the body," he said. "Where have you been?"

"We just came from the seventeenth heaven," Gabriel said.

"Seventeen me no seventeenths!" Blake exclaimed, his face flushing. "Mathematical form is death to the spirit. Only living form is truth. I will have no talk here of hierarchies or rankings."

"Now, now," Gabriel said, putting his hand on Blake's muscular forearm. "It's only a manner of speaking. We saw Dante there."

"And how is Messer Dante?" Blake said. The expression on his face was milder now. "A great genius, to be sure, but deeply entangled in Satan's labyrinth."

"Why do you think so?" I said.

"I do not *think* so," Blake said, "I *see* so. Dante's God is something vastly inferior to the Father of all mercies. For if He gives His rain to the evil and the good, and His sun to the just and the unjust, He could never have created hell. Whatever book speaks in favor of vengeance, and against the forgiveness of sins, is not of the Father."

"Dante is learning that, my dear," Gabriel said. "Slowly and painfully, but he is learning."

"I am glad of it," Blake said. "What is the joy of heaven, after all, but improvement in the things of the spirit? What are the pains of hell but ignorance, bodily lust, idleness, and devastation of the spirit? Men are not punished *for* their sins, but *by* them."

"If you wouldn't mind, Mr. Blake, would you tell me about *this* heaven?" I said. "Do people have to be Michelangelos or Isaiahs to enter? What about ordinary folks who have lived good, decent lives?"

"People are admitted into this heaven," Blake said, his eyes blazing, "not because they have curbed and governed their passions or have no passions, but because they have cultivated their understandings. The treasures of heaven are not negations of passion, but realities of intellect, from which all the passions emanate uncurbed in their eternal glory. The fool shall not enter into heaven, be he ever so holy."

"There are other heavens for fools," Gabriel whispered to me. "Actually, some of those heavens are quite interesting. It depends on the kind of fool."

"But Mr. Blake," I said, "why are you so severe with fools?"

"Because, sir, they are enemies of the imagination. This world of imagination *is* the world of eternity. It is the divine bosom into which we come after the death of the corporeal self. In it exist the permanent realities of everything which we once, with our finite organical perception, saw reflected in the vegetable glass of nature. Imagination is the divine body in every man."

"But doesn't it matter to you whether a spirit has been a good person or not?"

"That is no business of *mine*," he said. "I do not consider either the just or the wicked to be in a supreme state, but to be every one of them in states of the sleep which the soul may fall into in its deadly dreams of good and evil. Here people no longer talk of what is good or evil, or of what is right or wrong, and no longer puzzle themselves in Satan's labyrinth, but converse with eternal realities as they exist in the human imagination."

"And how do you converse with eternal realities?"

"Through the practice of my art, sir. Even in heaven, without unceasing practice nothing can be accomplished. If you leave off, you are lost. Ask any of my good friends over there," he said, nodding in the direction of the other table, "if he has not continued to grow in his art ever more passionately since the day of his death. Someday all people will come to be like us."

"How do you mean?"

"On the last day, the cherub with his flaming sword will leave his guard at the Tree of Life. And when he does, the whole creation will be consumed and will appear as it is: infinite and holy. This will come to pass by an improvement of sensual enjoyment."

"Sensual enjoyment?" I said.

"I'm sorry to interrupt," Gabriel said to me. "But we have to be on our way now."

"Wait, wait!" I said. "Just a little more. Please! We've barely gotten started."

"No, my dear, you're becoming too interested. I promised to bring you back. We really have to be going." And then, to Blake, "Goodbye. Till the next time. Give my love to Kate."

"I shall do that," Blake said. We all stood up. "And to you, sir," he said, bowing, "a very happy return to your body, and God bless you."

Gabriel took my hand.

I found myself in darkness. I was entirely comfortable, but I could no longer feel my spirit-body at all. There was nothing perceptible but a shimmer on the horizon of my awareness. I knew that this was Gabriel's voice, though the sensation was neither visual nor auditory. It was more intimate than that, as if the voice were amniotic fluid and I a fetus inside the womb.

"You will be returning to your body now," Gabriel said. "Do you understand yet?"

"I've *seen* a great deal. I don't know if I understand it."

"This is something that we should talk about when we return to earth. It's why I came to you."

"And why exactly is that?" I said.

"Because you are still holding on to the idea of a consciousness that is superior to your own."

"Aren't you supposed to be an archangel? You sound like a Zen Master."

"For your benefit," Gabriel said. "But truly, when I see an awakened one who has grown beyond all the heavens, I can only sigh with admiration."

For the briefest of moments the face of my teacher David appeared before me, projected in the darkness as if onto a movie screen. Everything I knew about him, and the whole history of our friendship, was present in that instant: a world in a grain of sand. I felt a rush of gratitude.

"Breathe now," Gabriel was saying. "Breathe . . ."

chAptEr V

WHAT DOES IT MEAN TO AWAKEN from
the mind's deadly dreams of good and evil? What is it
like to be someone who has grown beyond all the heavens? I can't speak from experience, but I can tell you in
greater depth about my teacher David Copland. David is
so much a part of who I am that it would feel incomplete
if I didn't include his story, which I think of as a more elegant version of my own, and a continuation of it. And if
I never wake up as thoroughly as he has, that is okay too.
His light doesn't have to shine from me for it to be mine.

I know David intimately, but he doesn't talk about his
personal life, and I've learned about his spiritual practice
only through many years of tactful prying. His insistence
on the essential is, I think, a measure of his impeccability

as a Zen teacher. It is also a measure of his transparency. In a poem called "Biography of the Awakened Masters" (the title is almost as long as the poem), he wrote:

> The story demands a plot.
> But there is no plot.
> That is the story.

He was born in Brooklyn in 1936, to assimilated, lower-middle-class, socialist parents. His paternal grandfather, whom he felt very close to, was an Orthodox Jew who at the age of sixty, after a successful career in garment manufacturing, retired to study the Talmud. When Grandpa Kaplan died in 1957, he left David three thousand dollars and a trust fund that yielded fifteen hundred annually. David was frugal enough to live on this money for the six years that followed his graduation from Columbia. In 1963, as he was completing his Zen training, he signed over the trust fund to his youngest brother and began to earn his living as a bookbinder, a trade he had learned during his college years because his grandfather had insisted on it. (The Talmud says that a father is obligated to teach his son three things: Torah, a trade, and how to swim; in this way, the boy is equipped for any eventuality life can bring him. David's father, being a good, upwardly mobile socialist, only provided for the swimming lessons. It was his grandfather who, more or less on the sly, taught him Hebrew and Torah.)

The first period of his life that he told me about in any detail was his nine-month-long stay in Jerusalem, which began in February, 1958. He went so that he could study with Martin Buber, the only modern Jewish thinker he respected. In spite of Buber's Teutonic ponderousness and the obscurity of his style, his books spoke to David's heart. One passage in particular affected him in a way that he couldn't understand, and finally moved him to write to Buber. This was a paragraph in *I and Thou* that describes an encounter with a cat. Buber looks into the cat's eyes and the cat looks back into his, with a glance that has been ignited by proximity to the human, a glance that asks, "Do you really mean *me*? Am I the one you are addressing? Are you really here for me? What is it that is coming from you? What is it that is around me? What *is* it?" The passage spoke deeply to David: not only the poignance of the experience, but also Buber's humility and humor (at least, this was the closest he got to humor) in placing a house cat in his pantheon of examples.

David told me several times how grateful he was for the kindness Buber showed him during that year. They met for an hour or so every Thursday afternoon in the study of Buber's old Arab-style house on Hovevey-Tsion Street. These conversations were the focal point of David's intellectual and spiritual life. He set the scene for me: on the walls an antique map of Jerusalem, a Piranesi etching of the Piazza Navona in Rome, and a photo of Buber's wife Paula; then the oil stove and the sofa where Buber used to take his late-afternoon naps; rows of tall, expensive art books on the glass-paneled shelves of the bookcases, along with Hebrew and German Bibles, sets of Goethe, Schiller, Heine, and the other German classics, all the major philosophers, and much of the rabbinic and Hasidic literature; Buber's three mercurial cats, any one of whom, at any moment, might suddenly leap in or out of an open window; the oak desk with the old-fashioned telephone on it and the magnifying glass he used for reading, the piles of books, manuscripts, letters, and page proofs; and across from David, always meeting and confronting him, Buber's beautiful, sad, white-bearded prophet-face.

For eight months the conversations proceeded as he had hoped they would, although he had imagined them as dialogues rather than the German-accented mono-logues they turned out to be. It was not that Buber didn't invite his thoughts and opinions. He did, and he listened carefully. But who could say anything that would stand up to Buber's astonishing eloquence? The words poured forth from his mouth like a mighty torrent. As they rushed by, David could barely think of his own ques-tions, much less his objections, the uncertain thoughts of an unformed young man of twenty-two. Nevertheless, he was thrilled simply to be in the presence of the great man. At the end of each session, Buber would assign him a passage from the Bible to study during the week, usu-ally from Genesis or the prophets. The following Thurs-day, invariably, after two or three minutes of David's tentative comments, Buber would open his mouth and the mighty river of Buberian eloquence would rush forth over David once more, and sweep him away.

Then, one chilly October afternoon, ten minutes into their meeting, Buber received an urgent phone call and had to leave the house. As he put on his overcoat, he said that David was welcome to wait in the study, in case he himself managed to return within the hour.

David picked an art book and sat down again in front of Buber's desk. At that moment one of the cats, a svelte black-and-gray female who had been curled on top of a bookcase, awoke, yawned, stretched, leapt down to the floor and up onto the desk (the only place in the room that was strictly out of bounds), and squeezed herself between two piles of books. David watched her light-footed maneuvers with interest. After she was finally settled, having given her right paw a few cursory licks, she looked up and met his eyes.

What happened next was completely unforeseen. He felt her gaze enter his as a knife enters a scabbard. Then there was only one gaze. He had become the cat or, more accurately, he had become a totality that included his limited, astonished human self and whoever it was that was staring at him through those black blade-thin slits. He took great pains to describe the feeling to me. (By the mid-eighties, I'd had my own touchstone experiences, so I was not in foreign territory.) It was, he told me, as if metal had touched metal and an electric circuit had been completed. The gaze ran from pole to pole and was everywhere along the circuit, neither cat's nor human's, and yet, at the same time, both. He was aware that he hadn't left his body: he could still feel his breath, his heart, could still place his attention in his hands or feet. But he could also feel the higher-pitched heart pulse of the cat, her animal hunger, her mischievous pleasure at sitting on the forbidden desk, her placid but formidable will, the intelligence thrillingly alive in her body, he could feel into her lithe tail, into her exquisitely sensitive tongue and her flickering intention to unsheathe her claws in pleasure. The intimacy was beyond anything he had thought possible. They were gazing in unison, breathing in unison.

Then, after a minute perhaps, the cat's attention was caught by a sound in the street; she looked away; the circuit was broken. Overjoyed and not a little shaken by this experience, David placed the book back in the bookcase and left.

The next meeting turned out to be a great disappointment. Buber was not pleased. He listened to David's account with weary eyes, using the cap of his fountain pen to make little hollow sounds as he tapped his right temple with its open end. When David finished, Buber shook his head and sighed. This kind of ecstatic experience, he said, pleasurable though it might be, could easily seduce a young person away from the centrality of the I-Thou relationship. It was of vital importance to recognize that such experiences are only experiences of the exclusive and all-absorbing unity of one's own self. The self appears to be so uniquely manifest, so uniquely existent, that the individual loses the sense of his separate individuality and interprets this awareness of his own unity as an experience of *the* unity. And when he returns to the wretchedness of daily turmoil, transfigured and exhausted, he is bound to feel that Being itself is split asunder, with one part abandoned to hopelessness. What help is it then to the soul that it can be transported again from this world into that unity, when the world itself has no share in that unity, and what does all enjoyment of God profit a life torn into two conflicting parts? If that luxuriantly rich heavenly moment has nothing to do with my poor earthly moment, what is it to me, as long as I must in all seriousness live on earth? What happened here was a marginal exorbitance of the act of relation: the relationship itself in its vital unity was felt so vehemently that the I and the Thou between whom it was established were forgotten. This is one of the dangerous phenomena that one finds on the margins where actuality becomes blurred, Buber said.

What David could understand of all this seemed untrue. He had had the experience. It was genuine. He didn't question its importance. It hadn't split him in two at all; on the contrary, he had returned to his everyday life with a sense of wonder, as if he had walked through a doorway into a deeper dimension of reality.

For the next month the conversations were uncomfortable, painful even, permeated as they were by the constant strain of conflict, even when they were centered on the weekly Bible passage. Buber was, of course, eloquent in his warnings against what he called the purveyors of unification and deniers of the self: mystics, the poets of the Upanishads, even the Buddha. For the first time David felt strong enough, stubborn enough, to argue. He was not going to have his experience whittled down by analysis, or fit into anyone's system of values, or called, as Buber wound up calling it, "an exalted form of being untrue." He began to suspect that when Buber spoke about the Upanishads or the Buddha, he was speaking ignorantly, perhaps from some unacknowledged fear of losing control. Much against his will, and with the embarrassment of a child who first sees the moral flaws of a much-loved, idealized parent, he began to suspect that Buber's God was a figment of that sincere, top-heavy, text-burdened intellect. Finally, on the second Thursday in November, Buber suggested that it was time to call an end to their meetings. He stood up and gave David his farewell blessing, a blessing heavy with grave concern and disapproval.

It was difficult, once David was back in New York, not to feel that Buber had failed him, and that he himself had failed to both honor his own experience and pay proper respect to the old man, who had received him with such generosity. He would have loved to keep sitting at Buber's feet, as so many others had done, in clouds of reverence and confusion. But Buber's own cat, perhaps a descendent of the very cat he had written about in *I and Thou*—but no, that one lived in Germany, in another, darker time—had led him in a different direction. David refused to believe that his experience was a delusion, that life even at its best was, as Buber had warned him, filled with the sublime melancholy of the fated lapse into It of every Thou. He kept feeling that there had to be something more.

There was.

2

The great transformation happened as the result of a lecture that D. T. Suzuki gave at Columbia two months later, in March. What riveted David to his seat was a passage Suzuki quoted from the great Japanese Zen Master Dōgen: "To study Buddhism is to study the self. To study the self is to forget the self. To forget the self is to be enlightened by all things." Although he knew he was only on the periphery of these words, he felt that they were resonant with a meaning that was vitally important for him. Somehow they referred to his encounter with Buber's cat, and he wanted to understand them more deeply. After the lecture, he approached Suzuki and asked him if there was an authentic Zen Master he could wholeheartedly recommend. Suzuki wrote down a name and address. David left for Japan a week later.

Tao-shan, the man who became David's teacher, taught in a remote monastery in the north of Japan. He was an unusual Zen Master: a celibate monk (the great majority of Japanese Masters are married), eccentric, rebellious, solitary, who had broken with tradition in an unheard-of way for a Japanese. According to him, both major schools of Japanese Zen—Rinzai and Soto—had so degenerated since their heyday in T'ang dynasty China, had so devalued their spiritual currency, that the title of Zen Master was now practically worthless. Though he had studied with skilled teachers from both schools, and both had given him Dharma transmission—certification that he had completed his training and was authorized to teach—his loyalty was to the ancient Masters from the golden age of Zen in China. The Chinese name he had taken after his great enlightenment was an acknowledgment and a testimony.

David told me very little about his introductory meeting with Tao-shan, except that he had presented himself in the interview room of the abbot's quarters, made his formal bows, talked with him for less than ten minutes, and been enlightened. Granted, this was only a first *ken-sho*, a glimpse into reality. But it was a powerful one. Tao-shan hadn't seen anything like it since his own experience some forty years before. The only account of it, as far as I know, is in two poems David wrote in 1989 for my son Jacob, who was a loquacious six at the time. Their import is, of course, beyond a child's grasp, but Jacob, and later my daughter Ruthie, loved the poems for their characters and their sounds. Here is "The White Rhinoceros," which, since it is gentler, David called his Soto version:

> I took a number 7 bus
> To see the White Rhinoceros.
>
> I rang the bell. He let me in
> And said, "Hello. How have you been?"
>
> I told him all my hopes and fears.
> He looked at me and flicked his ears.
>
> I told him all my fears and hopes.
> He handed me two telescopes.
>
> I questioned him about his horn.
> He said, "Before the world was born."
>
> "But how," I asked him, "can that be?"
> He said, "And now it's time for tea."
>
> I left his house at half-past-four.
> He chuckled as he shut the door.

"The Answer," which he called his Rinzai version, and which my children especially savored for its difficult words, is a more raucous account:

It was a bilgy, bulgy night
Inside the whiffle bog.
The ling-langs howled, obstreperous;
The owls, ambideperous,
Fell both ways through the fog.

I came condensed and dire of heart,
My pockets lined with glue.
I bowed; and stood there grinned-upon,
Aghast that I was pinned upon
A certain point of view.

I asked him why, I asked him whence,
I asked him whither-ho.
I asked him if my gravity
Would lift inside the Cavity
And where the greens would go.

He sat up in his velvet chair,
More silent than a sheep.
Perhaps he was considering
A way around my diddering;
Perhaps he was asleep.

I heard the owls go hooling past
The ling-langs' drizzling drone.
I heard the hippos' trumpetsound,
And camels with their crumpetsound
Together or alone.

"Wake up," I called, "salubrious sir."
"Wake up! Wake up!" he said;
And straighter than a chalkingstick,
He grabbed his rubber walkingstick
And hit me on the head.

A light went on inside my brain:
"Aha!" I cried with glee.
The world was bright and boisterous,
And I—released, rejoisterous—
Felt rounder than a pea.

And ever since that bulgy night
Inside the whiffle bog,
I've lived my days in clarity,
My evenings in hilarity,
As fragrant as a frog.

Shortly after David wrote the poems, I asked him about the meeting they were based on. I was too curious not to, though I also didn't want to pry too much. It was a delicate matter. I knew that he avoided talking about his several enlightenments, because such dramatic openings have a compelling power over students' minds: we invariably romanticize them and create mental images that get in the way of our own experience. But the fact that he wrote about this meeting at all, even though in the form of two children's poems, seemed to give me a certain permission to inquire. What I was most puzzled by were the discrepancies between the two accounts. For all its wackiness, "The Answer" has the classic lineaments that appear in a thousand ancient Zen stories. The transaction and especially the moment of enlightenment are less obvious in "The White Rhinoceros."

"It's clear," I began, "exactly when you have your experience in 'The Answer': 'A light went on inside my brain.' But when does it happen in 'The White Rhinoceros'?"

"When do you *think* it happens?"

"My guess would be, when the Master says, 'It's time for tea.' Pardon the rhyme."

"That's a good guess. But in fact, it happens before the world was born."

"Please, David. I'm just trying to get a handle on the experience."

"I'm being quite serious," he said, with a smile in his eyes. "Anyway, experience comes without a handle. You know that."

I knew how slippery a Zen Master can be: a cross between Jacob's angel and greased pig. "Let me start over again," I said. "Where in the poem does the speaker get enlightened?"

"He is on the brink of it during tea. The Rhinoceros sees his mind expanding like a balloon. It takes just one little pinprick. The sound of a chuckle, perhaps."

"He's so much subtler than the Salubrious Sir, who whacks the speaker over the head with that silly rubber walkingstick."

"The walkingstick is *not* silly. Not in the least."

"But walkingsticks aren't made of rubber."

"This one is."

"But if it's rubbery, how can it support him?"

"It can't. That's the point. When there's nothing to depend on, you can always walk on your own two legs. But it's very handy for whacking a student who should know better."

"A bit violent, though."

"It is an act of *love*."

"But the Rhinoceros's means are so much gentler."

"Yes, Tao-shan was like that. He could be as gentle as a woman's touch, yet five minutes later, or five days, you'd realize that he had walloped you right between the eyes."

Whatever the actual dialogue was, David awakened to his true nature during that first meeting with Tao-shan. He must have been extraordinarily ready.

3

Zen makes a useful distinction between "the man of talent" (nowadays this translates as "the man or woman of talent") and "the man of effort." In the end they are equal, and there are famous Masters of both types. But their processes are very different. The man of talent is rare. He is the delight of his teacher, because he makes the teacher irrelevant. The texts say that he is like a superior race horse, who runs even at the shadow of the whip. All he needs is a hint, and before long, instead of student and teacher, the two are colleague and colleague, friend and dear friend. Men of effort, like me, are much more common. We have to devote years, decades, to slogging in the muck, clearing and preparing the mind-soil, pulling up the roots of our delusions one by one, whereas the mind of a man of talent is already clear and fertile. He drops in an acorn and a month later it is a thirty-foot-tall oak tree, holding out its branches as a shelter for all the birds of the sky. In the earlier stages of practice, before I was capable of entirely rejoicing in the joy of others, I would sometimes sense, beneath my admiration, a barely subliminal grumbling when I read about someone like this, a soft resentful gnashing of teeth, as if some part of me was playing Salieri opposite his Mozart.

David trained in Japan for four years. Tao-shan had a monastery on a mountain in the far north of the main island of Honshu. It was a wild and beautiful setting for intensive Zen practice. The mountaintop had been cleared for the monastery's four buildings—meditation hall, dormitory for the ten monks, kitchen, and abbot's quarters—but the slopes were densely forested with pine and fir. A stream, whose song David spent many hours listening to, began near the top and descended the whole length of the mountain. Beside it, a seventeenth-century Paul Bunyan of a Zen Master had singlehandedly built a flight of rough granite stairs, hewing and carrying slabs that weighed hundreds of pounds apiece; he had spent fifty-three years on the project in order to make it easier for future monks to climb up and down, and had completed it when he was eighty-seven. Several hundred yards from the bottom of the stairs was the farming village that partially supported the monastery. Tao-shan would take his monks down the mountain one afternoon a week for a scalding soak in the communal bath, after which, with straight razors, soap, and bowls, they would shave one another's heads, two by two like Nausicaa and her maidens in *The Odyssey*, who sat by the river pool combing and braiding one another's long golden hair and anointing themselves with sweet oil. (Is this David's simile or mine? I can't remember.) On special occasions the villagers would invite them for a dozen-course vegetarian feast, where everyone would get royally drunk.

To say that David and Tao-shan recognized each other would be an understatement. Tao-shan had never seen anyone like David. During the thirty years of his teaching career, the monks he had trained had been hackers and duffers, decent journeymen students of the Way, with here and there a glimmer of understanding, or at most a shallow, uncultivated insight. David's talent, on the contrary, seemed unlimited. He had come to Tao-shan ripe to the bursting point. Their intimacy was instantaneous. (Language wasn't an obstacle, since Tao-shan spoke excellent English; in the 1920s, before he became a Zen Master, he had spent two years studying economics at Stanford.) Meeting David was, he later said, like falling in love. He was suddenly presented with a successor, a son. He hoped everything from this young foreigner's talent. Especially he hoped that David would complete the great work of Dharma practice, fully embody the wisdom of a buddha, and take it with him, *as* him, to America, for the benefit of all beings. When David had had his head shaved in order to be less conspicuous in the monastic setting, Tao-shan, looking with admiration at his high forehead and unusually large skull, had called him "the American Bodhidharma" (Bodhidharma being the monk who brought Zen from India to China in the fifth century).

Tao-shan was a demanding teacher, though no more demanding of David than David was of himself. The monastery schedule, famous for being one of the most rigorous in Japan, left little time for direct contact between them—when the monks weren't meditating, they were doing manual labor—except during formal interviews. During their meetings Tao-shan was sparing with his praise. But David didn't need praise. Tao-shan's pleasure and pride in him were written all over his face. When, two months after his arrival, Tao-shan gave him a rosary of twenty-four black coral beads and—far more precious—the patched and tattered traveling-robe that had belonged to *his* teacher and to his teacher's teacher, David understood that these gifts were an acknowledgment: however incomplete his realization seemed now, he was already an integral part of Tao-shan's tradition, and someday, when the part became the whole, he would be the seventy-ninth Master in this unbroken lineage that traced its origin through T'ang dynasty China back to the Buddha himself, wisdom pouring itself from mind to mind as water is poured from vessel to vessel, passing from heart to heart as a flame is passed from wick to wick through millennia of candles. Tao-shan also gave him a Dharma name: Mu-gaku, in Sino-Japanese. When David heard it for the first time, he laughed out loud. It meant "No Enlightenment": a terrific name to teach with. Many times, after he returned to America, people who had heard about it would ask its meaning and, when he told them, would, in their embarrassed, solicitous, uncomprehending way, try to make him feel better by saying, "Oh, that's too bad, but maybe someday you'll get there." And this would give him an opportunity to explain that "enlightenment" is just a word; it adds nothing to what is already present in each of us, shining beyond gain or loss. That is why the Buddha said, "When I attained Absolute Perfect Enlightenment, I attained absolutely nothing."

And why Dōgen wrote, in the continuation of the passage that had first struck David during the D. T. Suzuki lecture, "To be enlightened by all things is to drop off your own body and mind, and to drop off the bodies and minds of others. No trace of enlightenment remains, and this no-trace continues endlessly." You wash away the dirt, then you wash away the soap that washed away the dirt. You heal yourself of the disease, then you heal yourself of the medicine. What is left has nothing special about it. No Buddha (awakened being), no Dharma (teaching), no Sangha (community). It's just you, beneath the big sky of no enlightenment, treading the lush, bountiful earth of everyday mind.

One of the few conversations with Tao-shan that David ever quoted to me verbatim took place about six months after David began studying with him. Tao-shan said to him, "You have three jobs here. Your first job is to kill the buddha."

"I've already done that," David said.

"Prove it," Tao-shan said.

"We had a nice funeral," David said, smiling. It was a cat-that-ate-the-canary smile.

Tao-shan said, "Why didn't you invite me?"

David said, "If you had come, it wouldn't have been a funeral."

Tao-shan nodded. "Good." Then he said, "Your second job is to kill your father."

This took David aback. They had never talked about his parents, or indeed about anything personal. "What do you mean?" he said.

"As long as there is anything you want from your father," Tao-shan said, "or anything in him that you disapprove of, he will be an obstacle in your mind. 'Killing your father' means letting go of him completely; in other words, accepting him just as he is. He enters your mind like an image reflected on the water. No ripples."

"Ah. And my third job?"

"Is to kill me."

It took David four years to fully understand the gravity of these tasks, and another year and ten months to complete them.

Tao-shan's mind, David told me, moved with the indeterminacy of an electron. You could never tell where it was and how deadly fast it was approaching. Training with him was like training with a master swordsman: the slightest hesitation, the faintest flicker of discursive thought, and his mind, like a bamboo training-sword, came whistling out of nowhere to clobber you; even after David had developed enough agility to step out of its way, he was amazed at how close it would come, as if whizzing by and grazing a shoulder or an ear. During the next two years, while he was finishing the traditional koan curriculum and in their post-graduation meetings, he felt not only that he was learning how this mind moved, but that he was assimilating it, ingesting it, *di*gesting it in a kind of reverse digestion, letting his own mind become flesh of *its* flesh and bone of its bone. He wondered whether a greater intimacy could possibly exist, even between a husband and a wife. One particular koan, not in the official curriculum, became charged with meaning because it expressed a more advanced stage of what he was now experiencing:

A monk asked Ts'ao-shan, "What is a lion?"

Ts'ao-shan said, "The one no other animal can approach."

The monk said, "What is a lion's son?"

Ts'ao-shan said, "The one that devours its father."

The monk said, "If the lion is the one no other animal can approach, how can it be devoured by its son?"

Ts'ao-shan said, "When the lion's son roars, its father is devoured."

The monk said, "What happens to the lion's son after its father is devoured?"

Ts'ao-shan said, "The son completely dissolves into its father."

He saw himself steadily progressing toward this later stage. The more his realization of the truth deepened, the more his heart kept opening. His gratitude to and for Tao-shan was inexpressible.

On the sixth of May, 1962, he had his great enlightenment. He never talked about it, but he did show me a poem he had written shortly afterward, called "The Three Treasures":

Buddha
Wakes up, brushes teeth,
still the same old
face in the mirror.

Dharma
It costs a death:
what any
grass could tell you.

Sangha
No one in the audience
knows the bride or the groom,
yet we're all happy.

The exhilaration of the experience dissipated in a few
weeks, David said, but its effects were permanent. Actually, to call it an experience is misleading. All his previous
understanding fell away. There was no Zen left. There
was nothing but the glorious, wordless, essential fact.

Tao-shan recognized him immediately and was of
course overjoyed. Four months later, as a kind of per-
functory check, he asked David what his present viewpoint was. David said, unconsciously echoing the great
tenth-century Master Yün-men, "Exactly the same as the
viewpoint of all the ancient Masters."

"Wonderful," Tao-shan said. "But there is a further
step. Once, after Tung-shan gave a memorial service for
Yün-yen, his teacher, a monk asked him, 'Sir, do you
agree with the Master's teachings?' Tung-shan said, 'I
half agree and half don't.' The monk said, 'Why don't
you completely agree?' Tung-shan said, 'If I completely
agreed, it would be ingratitude to him.'"

David nodded.

"This is true ripeness," Tao-shan continued. "Zen Master Kuei-shan said that if your insight is equal to your
teacher's, you lack half his power. Only if your insight
surpasses your teacher's are you worthy to be his heir.
After you receive transmission, I would like you to wait
three years before you begin to teach. Let yourself deepen.
When you are ready, you'll know it."

The transmission ceremony was a splendid affair. His opinion of them notwithstanding, Tao-shan was much admired by his colleagues, and some of these Zen Masters, plus high government officials, corporation presidents, and assorted other big shots, attended from all over Japan. Aside from the incense and chanting and ceremonial horse-hair whisks and black robes and elaborate brightly-colored heavily-brocaded silk bibs, the occasion was surprisingly like David's Bar Mitzvah, peopled with doting, clucking uncles and aunts, punctuated by social hyperbole and useless gifts. But what was important had already happened.

After the ceremony, David left for a month-long solitary retreat at a hermit's hut near another monastery a few mountains to the west. He wanted to let everything settle and deepen further, in solitude, away from Tao-shan's other students, whom he had been living with in such close quarters, and whose awe or jealousy he continually had to sidestep. Tao-shan sent off a messenger to announce David's intention and to see that weekly provisions of rice and water would be left outside the hut. When the arrangements had been made, David set out, carrying a three-day supply of seaweed-rolled rice-and-pickle balls and wearing his great-grandteacher's patched, threadbare, priceless traveling-robe. Three hundred yards down the granite steps, he turned to look back. Tao-shan was still there, standing at the top of the mountain, waving goodbye.

4

The hermit's hut turned out to be a ramshackle affair
that hadn't been used in fifty years, but it suited David
perfectly. And in the glorious September weather, even a
roof over his head seemed superfluous. He had nothing
to do now, no one to please, nothing to attain. All beings
were already saved. The whole universe rested in the
palm of his hand. Each day seemed like a ripe fruit waiting on the branch for him to pluck it. Two weeks passed
like this. His sense of fulfillment seemed beyond joy and
sorrow.

At the beginning of the third week, he felt a stirring in
his depths, like the faint premonitory tremors of an
earthquake. It was a feeling of intense discomfort.

It took much effort, David told me, to stay with the
discomfort, an effort that felt peculiar to him, since he
had always found meditation so rapturously easy. It was
as if his consciousness were a vast scene—the clear sky,
the fullness of the earth, the world and they that dwell
therein—and in one corner of one small landscape a tiny
smudge appeared. The temptation was to merge into the
spaciousness of landscape or sky and let the smudge take
care of itself. But with persistence, he was able to focus on
it, to enter it.

It was located in his heart, this discomfort. It had no
content, or none yet. But David knew that it was not just
a transitory feeling, except insofar as all feelings are transitory. It was a condition. His heart was not yet fully at
peace. This was the truth. He had not yet completed his

work. He had gone through a great enlightenment, his beloved teacher had given him his seal of approval, he had become the seventy-ninth Master in their lineage, and his heart was not yet—he had to admit it—his heart was not yet fully at peace.

His first reaction was a fierce determination to complete the work. His second was rage.

The rage took him by surprise. He was not a person much given to anger. As a matter of fact, during his three and a half years of Zen practice, he had felt only a dozen momentary flashes of it pass through his body like shooting stars. This rage was different. It was like a bonfire, in fact like the cremation fire he had watched the year before at a comfortable distance, when a twenty-foot-tall mountain of logs had been set ablaze with the little black-robed corpse of a monk on top of it. Those flames were nothing, compared to the flames that he now felt inside him, starting in his solar plexus and roaring through his whole body.

Many thoughts and images passed in and out of the flames during the next, final two weeks of the retreat. He was furious at Tao-shan for giving him transmission prematurely, when he should have known that David's heart wasn't fully at peace. How could he, a man who called the Zen establishment corrupt, act with any but the highest possible standards in establishing his own succession? How could a teacher whose insight into the truth was so breathtakingly clear be sloppy in assessing the insight of his student? He had spoken so often about the requisite impeccability of a true Zen student, and yet at the moment when his own impeccability of judgment was most crucial, he had failed. Was it simply that he was blind to David's condition? Was his understanding of his students' karma so superficial? Or had he actually known how incomplete David was and had he—from a misguided compassion that was as corrupt as any laxness he had criticized in others, or from an ambition to succeed in America as quickly as possible—decided to hurry David along, hoping that the process would complete itself by the time David was ready to teach? These thoughts, and hundreds of variations on them, not only passed through the flames of David's rage, they were themselves flames that seared every part of his body and mind. There were images also, which kept springing up in the general conflagration, images of Tao-shan looking at him with contempt or with a simpering pride, images of himself spitting on the ground as Tao-shan walked by or of leaving the monastery in fury without saying a word. And when the rage let up for a while, he could feel, beneath it, layers of disappointment and grief. During these two weeks there were periods of calm, when he disengaged himself from all this mental and emotional activity and could see how excessive, how delusional it was. But most of the time he let the fire burn.

After the retreat, he returned to Tao-shan's monastery and requested an interview. As he bowed to the Master, he could feel the rage flaring up through his hands and eyes. Tao-shan registered it in his look. The change was subtle, but David could see him taking in the anger, his serene, amused expression intensifying for a moment.

David announced that he was leaving for America. He didn't mention that he was going back not as Tao-shan's successor and Dharma-heir but as a student without a teacher, a simple Zen student who had solemnly promised himself, however long it took, to complete the work of embodying the buddha mind. Tao-shan nodded his approval. He told David to come back and see him whenever he wanted.

Two days later, at a monastery not far from the road that was leading him south, David gave away his traveling-robe to an elderly monk who couldn't have had the slightest idea of its value. The monk bowed, said a polite Thank-you, rolled up the robe, and ambled off to the dormitory.

5

Three separate times David told me how he gave away his teacher's robe. It was a crucial image for him, an image both of pain and of maturation which, even thirty years later, he said, still sent a surge of emotion through him when he talked about it. The story was always the same, but he emphasized different details in each telling. On one occasion he described the precise moment, five minutes before the elderly monk happened to pass by, when he knew that he would have to get rid of the robe—not by returning it to Tao-shan, which would have been too unambiguous a gesture, a stark repudiation that he didn't mean and couldn't have meant, and not by taking it home, which would have been like hanging Nessus' shirt in the bedroom closet. Another time he described the monk's wrinkled face, magnified in the October sunlight, his surprise at David's offer, his peasant skepticism as he fingered the many-times-sewn-and-oversewn robe, which might still be good for another ten winters' use. In all the retellings, David's emotion was palpable. And I, as I listened, felt a mixture of deep sympathy for the young man he had been and relief at his initiation into difficulty and sorrow on the path, a not entirely altruistic "Welcome to samsara, pal" kind of identification. Looking back at the event was, he told me, an experience in which remembered grief and present tranquility were mixed like wine in water. It was like watching a sad, exquisitely made film in which he was both principal actor and canny auteur: the final glimpse of the beloved's face as she steps into the shadows; the last deep-red maple leaf snapping off from the branch and slowly, breathlessly, spiraling down to the chilled earth.

It took him two and a half years to complete this final part of his training. It was as painful as a divorce, he said. It *was* a divorce, if divorce can take place within the context of an indissoluble union. He had, in some temporarily devastating way, lost the person he most loved and trusted. Not that he ever stopped loving Tao-shan or felt anything less than gratitude for what that dear, extraordinary man had taught and untaught him. It was strange, he told me, to feel such love coexisting with his volcanic anger, like two blood-enemies who secretly are mirror forms of each other. Often, after he returned to America in October, he would shake his head in frustration at his interior scriptwriter for creating such a ridiculous melodrama. The only thing that carried him through the pain was his trust in the process.

By the end of November it had become obvious that much of his anger at Tao-shan was displaced anger at his own father. Once he saw this, he realized that he had essential work to do in a psychotherapeutic mode. Tao-shan had spotted it: "Kill your father, then kill me." David opened his bookbinding business so that he could pay for this work, which took him a year, from late February of 1963 to early March of 1964. But even though he must have moved through it with the speed and elegance of a man of talent, the process was, he said, a mortifying experience at first: here he was, the great Tao-shan's son and heir, the Buddha's seventy-ninth direct successor, the American Bodhidharma, starting back at square one, in the psychological cleanup brigade, incapable of saving anyone but, perhaps, himself. Instead of high spiritual drama, this was slapstick. He had stepped off the top of the hundred-foot flagpole, smack into a brick wall. He sometimes thought, wryly, that the chapter title for this year of his life would have to be "Buddha on the Couch" or, even more accurately, "Buddha on the Skids." It was absurd. It was necessary. It was hard work. And what had he attained as son and heir? What had there ever been to attain? Wasn't his mortification just a subtle form of clinging, a way of holding himself back from the process and not descending into grief with everything he could call his own? And wasn't this work life itself in all its superb rawness, no less spiritual than any other stage of his practice?

The specifics of the work he never told me. He just

mentioned that it occurred in the deeper darknesses of the unconscious and that it was like gardening: when you found a weed, you had to dig the roots out completely, leaving not even the tiniest hair-thin tip.

According to conventional Zen storytelling, all this couldn't be happening. You had your great enlightenment and that was it. You lived happily ever after, you filled out the fifty-year postscript, you walked all over India, or Iowa, with gift-bestowing hands and spoke-marks on the soles of your feet, teaching the truth, sharing the wealth. But enlightenment meant *finito*: that's all, folks. There was no such thing as post-enlightenment practice.

Obviously, David realized, this was just a way of shaping a biography, of making a more profound and textured adult story into a fairy tale that was both inspiration and obstacle for beginners on the path. He had no problem tossing out the Zen conventions. After all, the core of the tale was true. There *was* such an experience as a final awakening, it *was* possible to put an end to suffering, to feel any pain in the foreground of consciousness against a background of perfect repose. He knew that he had only to look inside himself to find the truth, immediately, beyond the categories of enlightenment and delusion. The essence of all scriptures was vividly spread out before him. He didn't have to turn a page. Could an enlightened person feel anger? Duh. Could an enlightened person be stuck in delusion? Yes: with awareness, for a while. How you knew when you had flushed out all the delusion was still unclear to him, but that by the end of the process it would be possible to know was never in question.

One of the dangers in using loaded words like "buddha" and "enlightenment," David found, was the idealization that almost necessarily comes along with them as part of the package. That was one reason he came to value the Tao Te Ching so highly, with its matter-of-fact insistence on the ordinariness of the Master, who makes mistakes just like the rest of us but is impeccable in admitting them as soon as he can see them and in correcting them with a minimum of karmic residue. The old Zen Masters were, of course, quite aware of the danger. His favorite among them, the golden-tongued, magnificently subtle Chao-chou, once said to a large audience, "Even the word 'buddha' makes me want to throw up." A monk stood up and asked, "Then how do you teach people?" Chao-chou said, "Buddha! Buddha!" Such meticulous teachers these old boys were. The pool was perfectly limpid: why stir up the mud?

And when it came to the emotional life of a buddha, it was easy to sleepwalk through a thicket of idealizations. Is the buddha-mind a place of absolute serenity, in which no thinking occurs and no "negative" emotions, nothing but benevolence, compassion, sympathetic joy, and equanimity? In one sense, yes. David knew that those qualities characterized the rediscovered, natural, and constant functioning of his own mind. But the passions were there as well, with their own truth, their own radar, their own *com*passion, which penetrated far beyond the reach of the conscious mind. There was such a thing as bodhisattva anger, for example. What would be the point of restricting yourself, using only the letters up to M in the alphabet of experience, castrating yourself of the body's intelligence, drying up the springs of grief or lust for the sake of a tranquility that is only half-alive? His favorite dialogue at the time once again starred Chao-chou:

Chao-chou said to the assembly, "Buddhahood is passion, and passion is buddhahood."
A monk stood up and said, "In whom does buddha cause passion?"
Chao-chou said, "Buddha causes passion in us all."
The monk said, "How can we get rid of it?"
Chao-chou said, "Why should we get rid of it?"

This last line was wicked in its kindness and, in the context of a conventional Buddhism that taught the extinguishing of desire, exquisitely funny.

In the early days of his Zen practice, David had thought that being beyond sorrow and joy meant that you wouldn't feel either emotion. He saw now that this was a misconception. Being beyond sorrow and joy meant immersing yourself in them completely, with your whole heart, in the midst of a boundless equanimity. Again, he found a Zen dialogue (he had studied it with Tao-shan) that perfectly expressed this point:

A monk asked Tung-shan, "When heat and cold come, how can we escape from them?"
Tung-shan said, "Why don't you go to the place where there is neither heat nor cold?"
The monk said, "What place is that?"

Tung-shan said, "When it is hot, you die of heat. When it is cold, you die of cold."

His anger continued to burn. He intended to keep standing in the midst of the flames, for as long as it took.

6

In May of 1964 David returned to Japan. His agenda was simple: to bow to his teacher. He had decided to do this once a year, as a kind of spiritual practice, for as long as Tao-shan was alive. He didn't expect anything to change.

After the bus dropped him off at the village, he spent an hour walking up and down the sloping, stone-paved streets. It felt odd to revisit this setting, after such profound changes inside and out, in jeans now instead of robes, and with hair on his head. Everything seemed familiar but askew, as if he were walking through a lucid dream in which he had come back as a reverse prodigal son, having deepened his substance with mindful living. The farmers were out in the fields. The village wives went about their chores or stood minding their children or gossiping at the well. Nobody recognized him.

As he climbed the huge granite steps, a sense of oppression settled onto his heart. He could feel it as an almost physical weight. He was having trouble breathing. He couldn't seem to take in enough air. Each exhalation ended in an involuntary sigh. By the time he reached the primitive outhouse halfway up the mountain, grief was pounding at every orifice of his body. He vomited before he could get inside, then had just enough time to pull down his pants, squat over the latrine hole, and spatter the pit with liquid feces. It took him half an hour to wash in the stream and compose himself.

At the top of the mountain, Tao-shan was in his room. David entered and did his usual three full prostrations. When he had finished and looked into Tao-shan's eyes, he could still feel the anger in his own heart. Nothing had changed. There was nothing to be said.

They made polite conversation for a few minutes. Tao-shan didn't ask why David had come or how long he planned to stay. "And this is how it will end," David thought. He would return to Japan every year. He would climb the mountain and bow to his teacher and the anger would still be there and he would bow again and leave. Until someday Tao-shan would die and David would return one last time and bow to an empty cushion, with the immeasurable gratitude and grief that he was feeling now. And he would have the rest of his life to complete the unfinished business.

After the interview was over, he walked back down the mountain and returned to Berkeley.

7

To support his psychic weeding, David also did some digging in classic Zen literature. There *were* a few, a very few, hints about post-enlightenment training that the old Masters had let fall, casually, in passing. These turned out to be helpful markers along the path, confirmations of what he already knew. He collected them and later had them printed in a little cardboard-bound manual (it measures five inches by six) for me and his other two students. Here are the first few pages of dialogues, with his comments in italics. Even if the words themselves don't mean much to you, I hope you can sense the kindness and the freedom from which they arise:

A monk asked Kuei-shan, "Does someone who has attained enlightenment still need to continue with self-cultivation?" *[Even to ask the question means that he's starting to wake up from his buddha dream.]*

The Master said, "Through meditation a student may attain thoughtless thought, become suddenly enlightened, and realize his original nature. *[Yay!]* But there are still delusions that have accumulated over numberless kalpas and cannot be purified in a single moment. *[The simple truth.]* Therefore he should be taught how to eliminate the karmic tendencies and mental habits. *[The whole challenge is in this how.]* There is no other way of cultivation."

———

A monk asked Chao-chou, "What is the essence of Zen?" *[The big question. "What is God?" "What am I?"]*

Chao-chou said, "Have you finished your cereal?" *[Breakfast time. But this also means "Have you completed the great work?" "Have you eaten your teacher?"]*

The monk said, "Yes." *[What unassuming confidence! Or is he just talking about his oatmeal?]*

Chao-chou said, "Then wash your bowl." *["But there's nothing to wash!"—"That's precisely why you have to wash it."]*

The monk's mind opened. *[I am very happy for you.]*

———

Once, when he was a young monk, Tung-shan said to his teacher Yün-yen, "I have some karma that is not yet eradicated." *[He strips himself naked in the town square.]*

Yün-yen said, "What are you doing about it?" *["Don't just do something: sit there" would clearly be a disaster. He'd better do something! But it can't be done by doing.]*

Tung-shan said, "I haven't concerned myself with the Four Noble Truths." *[Good. Why take the long way around?]*

Yün-yen said, "Are you joyful yet?" *[Ecstasy loves company.]*

Tung-shan said, "It's not that I'm not joyful. It's as if I have gotten hold of a pearl in a pile of shit." *[Eeeuuw! But there's no remedy for it. Later on, after you cart the shit out to the garden, the pearl will shine by itself. Wash your bowl! Save the whales!]*

———

Shen-shan was mending his clothes with a needle and thread. *[When you mend your robe, you're mending mine. Thank you so much.]*

Tung-shan said, "What are you doing?" *[Invitation à la danse.]*

"Mending." *[Everyday mind, so simple that all things turn into metaphor.]*

Tung-shan said, "How are you mending?" *[How is both lock and key.]*

Shen-shan said, "One stitch after the next." *[A tortoise answer. You can't get there from here.]*

Tung-shan said, "We've been companions on the path for twenty years now, and you can still say such a thing!" *[Fearless. This kind of honesty can come only from the best of friends.]*

220

Shen-shan said, "How do *you* mend?" *[A big fat bo-dhisattva lob.]*

Tung-shan said, "As if the whole earth were spewing flames." *[If not I, who? If not now, when?]*

———

Pai-chang taught the assembly, "The Sutra says, 'To behold the buddha nature you must wait for the right moment and the right conditions. When the time comes, you are awakened as if from a dream. *[Ahh. Coffee brewing. Toast in the toaster.]* You realize that what you have found is your own and doesn't come from anywhere outside.' *[Nor does it come from inside. That's what makes it your own.]* An ancient patriarch said, 'After enlightenment you are still the same as you were before. There is no mind and there is no truth.' *[The good news. The beloved's face.]* You are simply free from unreality and delusion. *[Summer morning: blue sky, ants in the kitchen.]* The ordinary person's mind is the same as the sage's, because Original Mind is perfect and complete in itself. *[Of course! 'Have some more apple pie.'—'Thanks, don't mind if I do.']* When you have arrived at this recognition, please hold on to it." *[Please don't hold on to it.]*

8

David finished this stage of his inner work on the tenth of April, 1965. He was twenty-nine years old.

It was an extraordinarily sweet moment. He realized that he was giving himself his own seal of approval, his own transmission of the Dharma. And he remembered one of the most moving lines in *The Divine Comedy*, the verse that signals Dante's spiritual graduation, in which Virgil says, *"te sopra te corono e mitrio"*: "I crown and miter you over yourself." He was standing in the same place that his dear Chao-chou had stood in—without that lightning-fast wit, to be sure, but with the same certainty, with no before or after, vastly, blessedly alone in the vast universe:

> A monk asked Chao-chou (whose Dharma name was Ts'ung-shen), "Master, who gave you transmission of the Dharma?"
> The Master said, "Ts'ung-shen."

And after all, what was this mind that had been handed down over the centuries? The simplest thing in the world. When a monk asked Chao-chou's teacher Nan-ch'üan, "What is it that is transmitted from Master to Master?" Nan-ch'üan answered, "One, two, three, four, five."

He returned to Tao-shan's mountain on May fifteenth. As he lifted his head from the third prostration in front of his teacher, he was aware that his anger had vanished, completely. His heart was weightless, it was overflowing, the whole room was filled with a palpable light. He looked into Tao-shan's eyes and laughed, Tao-shan laughed, they stood up, David took a few steps through light as dense as mist, they embraced. It was an embrace beyond his most extravagant dreams of resolution.

By the end of 1967 he felt ready to teach.

" **b**REATHE. BREATHE," Gabriel was
saying.

An electric current shot through me. I gasped and
swallowed air, my heart began to pump with a hammer
thud, my body poured sweat. I was aware now that I was
lying on my back under the walnut tree. A stone was digging into my right shoulder blade.

Ten minutes or so passed. After my breathing had become regular, I sat up.

"Are you all right?" Gabriel said.

"I think so."

He looked me over. "Why don't we take a walk?" he
said. "It will ground you."

We walked onto the paved driveway and slowly

around, in silence. It's a pleasant walk. Lots of trees, mostly black oak, live oak, and Monterey pine, and, separating the property from the road, a tall row of eucalyptus. To the right, before the driveway begins to curve, there's an acre of meadow with a little orchard at the far end: a couple of fig trees, the small apple tree, an apricot and a damson plum, and half a dozen prolific cherry-plums. We walked over the little wooden bridge that spans the creek, to the front gate with its iron grapeleaves and bunches of iron grapes, then turned and went back over the bridge, in silence. A few hundred yards farther on, we passed the almond and the birch tree, the blue-flowering rosemary and the blackberry bushes. On top of the car, in his New-York-Public-Library-lion pose, Magellan was waiting for us, or for me. He lifted his head and made that barely audible, croaking meow of his. I couldn't help going over and petting him with a few of his favorite strokes: under his chin, at the opening of his ears, up along the ridge of his nose, and sideways from his nose across his whiskers and cheekbones. He has a fine, gentlemanly purr.

We walked again, past the peach and walnut trees, the willow and persimmon, the big olive tree in the middle of the deck, the wild grapevines, and came around to the studio.

"How are you doing?" Gabriel said as we sat down.

"Better, thanks. I'm here."

"Good."

"How long were we gone?"

"Three minutes and forty-seven seconds," he said. "I counted."

"Holy mackerel!" I said. "It felt like years."

"It *was* a good tour, though you got just the briefest glimpse of the angelic heavens. Anyway, I hope it was instructive."

"It certainly gives me a lot to chew on. And thanks so much for getting me back on time."

"You're welcome. I did promise, after all. And there's a certain fascination that angels feel in adjusting ourselves to the scale of the human. We *can* keep track when we set our minds to it."

"Minutes and seconds must seem like very small potatoes to you."

"We find it more natural, of course, to think in terms of eons and kalpas, in which the birth and death of a universe is a passing incident. But it's a pleasure to fit into this marvelous body, to sit under these graceful, leafy creatures and feel your lives flowing by so very quickly. I, for one, am enchanted by everything human."

"'Eternity is in love with the productions of time.' Dear Blake."

"It's true that human time has something particularly charming about it, since, like the human body, it is exactly halfway between the infinitely large and the infinitesimally small. Though your science, in its present primitive state, doesn't have any idea *how* small or large a scale even physical reality functions on."

"Really?"

"Oh, you've barely started to scratch the surface," he said. "You're still laboring under the belief, for instance, that nothing moves faster than the speed of light."

"Ah."

"I rest my case."

"Still," I said, "what a joy it was to meet Blake. I wish I had asked him to read something he's working on now. If only I'd had more time." I thought of my conversation with him in that passionate, crystalline heaven, and of my other favorite heaven, where I had talked with Mozart over a cup of whipped-cream-topped hot chocolate. A string quartet on the front lawn had played his inexpressibly lovely quartet number three thousand and something. "And I would have liked to meet John Milton as well. The other Milton."

"I've paid Milton a number of visits over the centuries. He's much mellower these days."

"I'm glad. How about his work?"

"He still has the finest ear of all your poets. But he's writing about more essential matters now."

"*Paradise Lost* does seem awfully limited," I said, "in a strictly spiritual sense."

"Yes," Gabriel said, "he has told me more than once how embarrassed he was by that aspect of it just after he died. Cosmic war, spiritual wickedness in high places, salvation and damnation . . ."

"It *is* an incredible melodrama, amid all the magnificence of his language. Satan's a powerful character, though."

"But for whom?"

"Ah," I said. "Yes, I see your point. I suppose readers can't feel the full impact of the sexual *frisson* unless they've got that old-time religion. How can the figure of a cosmic rebel titillate if a cosmic king seems unreal? There's a deeper insight in *Job*, I think, where Satan's a member of the heavenly court."

"That *is* a nice touch."

"Oh, Satan is a member in excellent standing, who's just doing the Lord's work. But his true name is Lucifer, you know, 'bringer of light.' And maybe he's so attractive in *Paradise Lost* because we instinctively recognize the positive quality of his pride. 'I shall not serve.' Once you take away the resentment, that's really a declaration of spiritual independence. The kingdom of God is within *me*."

Gabriel smiled. "It's true. He would certainly live in our heaven, a most worthy opponent, if he existed." And then, after a pause, "How strange this belief in devils is. As if a heaven implied a hell."

"I sometimes think it's people's way of not being angry at God," I said. "You heap all the world's misery onto the bad guy, and that lets you see God as blameless. Ineffectual, but blameless."

"But don't they realize that the more you believe in the devil, the less you can love God?"

"No, they accept the whole package of opposites."

"It's a pity that humans concoct a cosmic opponent," he said, "when in reality God's grace is the beginning, the middle, and the end. When you pray for God's grace, you are like someone standing neck-deep in water and crying out for water. It's like saying that a fish in water feels thirsty, or that water feels thirsty."

"It can be distressing to feel that thirst, though."

"But it's just an optical illusion."

I remembered the time when I didn't know that. My thirst had felt very real.

We sat in silence for a few minutes.

"I told you that I had an agenda for this conversation," Gabriel said.

"Yes," I said. "Something about consciousness."

"And then I should be going."

"I really didn't mean to be rude by imposing a time limit. It's just that I have a date."

"I understand. But there's no need for me to stay any longer. We know each other. We have met."

"We have."

"There is still one thing about angels . . ."

"Yes?"

"You know it, but you're not fully conscious of it yet."

"Tell me."

"Let me ask you a question first: If you could change anything in your past, what would it be?"

I thought of the most painful experiences I'd ever gone through: a serious accident that my little girl barely survived, rocky periods of my marriage when Elizabeth was growing and I refused to budge, the deaths of close friends, those many years wrestling with the problem of evil. I had come to accept them all, with difficulty, with gratitude.

"No," I said, "there's nothing I would change. It's all very good."

"I thought you would say that," Gabriel said, smiling. "How wonderful."

"And you?"

"Ah. This, of course, is the point."

"What is?"

"Angels can't feel regret, because it's a mode of sorrow. But my admiration for you humans is a variation of regret, like a melody transposed from a minor to a major key."

"But regret for what? And what does it have to do with *us*?"

"There is a moment before creation . . . No, let me try saying this in a different way. There is a moment before every birth, when the unformed spirit pauses on the brink of becoming. Behind it, the vast unknown out of which it arises. In front of it, pure world."

"I'm sorry," I said, "may I interrupt? Is what you are saying a parable or is it literally true?"

"Oh, it's true. *And* it's a parable."

"Okay. Just checking. Please go on."

"The unformed spirit pauses on the brink of becoming. And, out of love and recklessness and the magnetic need to complete itself and a high curiosity, it is drawn to a life."

"Would you mind if I interrupted you again?"

"Not at all."

"You're saying that the spirit is drawn to a life. But at this point it's already a spirit, a separate being. So hasn't it already *become* something?"

"You're quite right," he said. "I'll explain that. And it's true that what I'm describing sequentially is an event that has no sequence: it's all enfolded within the single flash of a timeless instant. So in this sense what I'm telling you is a parable. But for the sake of the reality it expresses, let me focus on the transition."

"Okay."

"The spirit sees a self and becomes it. It may take on the longest or shortest of lives, a life of bliss or deprivation or horror. It may become—I'll use examples that you'll recognize—a mosquito or a sequoia or an electron or a human being. Or it may become an archangel."

I nodded.

"Before it plunges into a physical or a non-physical universe, the spirit is granted complete foreknowledge of the life it is about to enter. Not only foreknowledge, but since knowledge and power are one, it is granted complete choice. It sees everything displayed before it, as if on a movie screen, but collapsed into a less-than-an-instant. And it chooses everything. Suppose it feels drawn to the human world: it sees a mother and father whose giant shadows it will have to grow beyond if it can, like a plant reaching for light; a set of core puzzles that may take it a lifetime to resolve; sufferings and joys, opinions, obstacles, illnesses, triumphs, disasters, swirls of events that at first or at tenth glance seem trivial or accidental; a particular era and country, with their collective blindnesses; lovers and children; enemies, friends; the circumstances, terrified or serene, of a death. It chooses that whole life, down to its smallest detail. And since the spirit is one with the will of God, God's creation and its creation are the same."

"In other words," I said, quoting Yeats, "it knew at first what it learns at last: 'that it is self-delighting, / Self-appeasing, self-affrighting, / And that its own sweet will is Heaven's will.'"

"It knows. And then, at the moment when sperm pierces egg, it plunges headlong into the forgetfulness of the amniotic sea."

"A nice parable. But what connection does it have with your . . . regret, if I may call it that?"

"I am thinking of the point where parallel lines meet, where time curves into a circle, so that past and future are facets of the same jewel. If I had it to do all over again, as eventually I will, my choice would be different."

"Really? You wouldn't be an archangel?"

"No. Hovering on the edge of a life, so many kalpas ago, I would let myself be drawn to the human realm."

"You would? Wow!"

"Of course, I'm vastly grateful for being what I am. But when your life has been one of perpetual and unadulterated bliss, gratitude extends only so far. It is nothing like the gratitude a human being can feel."

"I'm astonished," I said. "That would never have occurred to me."

"Oh, I could sing for a very long time in praise of the human. Not only of the enlightened ones and the great artists, but of the mediocre and the tawdry. You are all beautiful."

"I'd love to hear one of those songs, someday. But if you don't mind holding off, I think it would be too much for me right now. I'm still taking in my *first* experience of angel music."

"Or I could list your virtues for you, courage being one

of the foremost among them. You are so ready to plunge into becoming, and so very often. It quite amazes us."

"What do you mean, 'so often'?"

"I'm speaking about the many spirits who, after one death, return to another body."

"Ah."

"It takes great courage," he said, "after all the sorrows and disappointments of one life, to enter a womb again. Not all of you do."

"How so?"

"Well, you might say that most of the heavens are waiting rooms for those who need to recover from a particular life."

"R and R?"

"Something like that. A moment of bliss, or a kalpa, and they are ready to try again."

"And three billion kalpas of bliss?"

"Yes, it does make you wonder, doesn't it? Perhaps I needed this life to recuperate from a previous one. I don't remember what came before. It might have been very difficult."

"So during the time you have been an archangel," I said, "I may have lived a zillion different lifetimes, in a zillion different bodies?"

"Perhaps."

"And before you chose to be an archangel?"

"Who knows what vast stretches of time preceded that? Or how many previous creations there were before this one in which we live and move and have our being?"

"And after your archangelic momentum peters out, what then? Will you be reborn as an earwig or a cat?"

"Perhaps."

"And does this round of births and rebirths go on forever?"

"No, there is an ultimate completion."

"Do you mind if *we* stop for a moment?" I said. "I've got to ask you. Is this the truth?"

"Yes, it is."

This was another interesting surprise. I hadn't expected to hear about reincarnation from the mouth of an archangel. Of course, I had encountered that teaching many times before, first in the kabbalistic literature I had studied with Reb Zusya, then in Hayim of Verona's *Etz Hayim*, then in the elementary, basic-Buddhism part of my curriculum with Sumi-sahn, who would always pooh-pooh it. "Very low-class teaching," he would say, wrinkling his nose. "*What* is reborn? What dies? *That* is the primary point."

"Well," I said to Gabriel, "with your permission, I'll take this as a parable."

"But I mean it quite literally. This is the way things are."

"It's not that I disbelieve you. Though I don't believe you either, if I may say that without disrespect. But I don't want to settle onto any idea, however reasonable it may sound."

"You may believe whatever you wish," he said. "I don't mind."

"It's nothing personal. I trust you very deeply, you know."

"I know."

"But a lot of my inner training has been on precisely this point. To keep the mind open to all possibilities."

"Oh?"

"And my teacher has paid particular attention to clearing out my flotsam and jetsam about death. He says that death is, literally, unthinkable. The mind has no way of grasping it. It isn't even an 'it.' Once we're dead, pure mystery takes over. I wouldn't want to limit the mystery by shaping my expectations to anyone's ideas, even an archangel's."

"But I can tell you exactly what happens," he said. "It's as simple as ABC. And you've seen it yourself. The spirit leaves the body and enters the realm of transitions. It sees the primal light . . ."

"I know, I know. But as much as I appreciate the tour, I don't take it as a preview. I'd rather keep my mind free of expectations. The more completely we move beyond our ideas about death, David says, the more open we are to the mystery at the heart of the universe. I hope you don't mind."

Gabriel smiled. "Not in the least."

"But getting back to your agenda, I still don't really understand why you would choose to become human. Could you elaborate?"

"Everything is God's grace," he said, "and I don't question the rightness of my choice at that moment so long ago. I remember it, though not so clearly as I remember the events of my life. I remember the disparate elements of archangelic consciousness drifting together, like a cloud forming in the empty sky. And then I was aware that an 'I' was taking place, and I was being drawn toward a most beautiful rose-colored light. I saw my etheric image like someone leaning over a pool and seeing his own face for the first time. I loved what I saw, loved the expanse of this life, the glow of this intelligence, the lovemaking, the creations. Then I felt myself being drawn into that light. It was like falling into the most pleasurable of dreams."

"Ah."

"And it *has* been pleasurable. More than pleasurable: blissful, supremely blissful, and every moment of every kalpa I give thanks to the great *I Am* for this consciousness. And yet . . ."

"And yet?"

"There is something more."

"Does it have to do with the ultimate completion that you mentioned? You were saying that the round of births and deaths doesn't go on forever."

"Yes," he said. "I can't tell you about this from my own experience. Nor can pure intellect arrive at an answer. And even about how I became an archangel, I have only a partial memory. At that moment, as you pointed out, I was already a separate being, a 'something' about to become something else."

"A One about to become a Two?"

"You could say that, yes. The *I Am* was speaking me into existence. Before the first number, after the last number: that is the realm of completion, the moment beyond creation, where the *I Am* is pure being, neither *is* nor *is not*."

"But if you haven't experienced this," I said, "and your intellect can't grasp it, how do you know?"

"I won't say that I know. But I believe that it's true. I have it on very good authority."

"Whose?"

"A teacher whom I visited once. A human being, in fact. A German. All honor to him."

"Who was it?"

"Eckhart," he said. "Do you know him?"

"*Meister* Eckhart? Yes, I do know his works, pretty well."

"That's right, I remember now. He appears in *Against Angels*."

"Briefly. He *is* a wonderful teacher. How did you come to visit him?"

"Oh, I never know how these things happen. I just felt one of those magnetic pulls into time that arise from time to time. They come out of nowhere, and I always follow. It was a very powerful attraction."

"And . . . ?"

"The whole encounter was as vivid as it could be," he said. "It seems like yesterday. It might have *been* yesterday, though according to your linear time I found myself in the early fourteenth century. He was sitting in his study: a slim, elegant man wearing a black robe over a white habit. To his right, there was a set of arched and latticed windows through which the morning light streamed in. He was at his desk, writing on a parchment scroll with a long feather. I didn't put on wings, of course. It would have been inappropriate."

"And how did he respond to you?"

"When he saw me, he briefly bowed his head, then went back to his writing. He was in a rapture, obviously. Yet his eyes weren't clouded over with a mystical glaze, like the two saints I have visited."

"Which ones?"

"I don't want to mention any names. But Eckhart seemed utterly alert. I stood facing him, and the words formed inside me as he formed them on the scroll. 'When I was in my first cause,' he wrote, 'I had no God, and I was cause of myself.' I had to gasp with astonishment."

"It must have been quite a shock," I said. "Eckhart can be very far-out."

"But it was written with absolute reverence," Gabriel said. "He *knew*. And I realized that these words, which arose from an understanding I couldn't begin to fathom, these words that describe what we all are before we are created and after the ultimate completion, were exactly what I had been waiting for, though I hadn't known I was waiting. I stood there, myself enraptured, awe-dazzled at each new depth."

"What came next?"

"'I lacked nothing,' he wrote, 'and I desired nothing, for I was an empty being and a knower of myself, rejoicing in the truth.' 'Yes,' I said to myself, 'that is truly how it must be.'"

"It does have a nice ring to it."

"And the rest explains and deepens it. 'I wanted myself and wanted no other thing,' Eckhart wrote. 'What I wanted I was, and what I was I wanted, and thus I was empty of God and of all things. But when I went out, by my own free will, and received my created being, then I had a God; for before there were creatures, God was not "God": he was simply what he was. But when creatures came to be and received their created being, then God was not "God" in himself, but he was "God" in the creatures.' Here, I remember, Eckhart paused for a moment to scratch his nose."

"Good for him," I said. "It's not easy to stay in your body in such exalted states."

"He scratched his nose, then began writing again. 'Now God,' he wrote, 'insofar as he is only "God," is not the ultimate goal of creatures. For the least of creatures *in* God has just as great a position. And if it were possible that a fly had intelligence and could with its mind search the eternal abyss of divine being out of which it came, we would have to say that God, with everything he is as "God," would be unable to fulfill or satisfy that fly. Therefore let us pray to God that we may be empty of "God," and that we may grasp the truth and eternally rejoice in it, there where the highest angels and the fly and the soul are equal, where I was pure being, and wanted what I was, and was what I wanted.'"

"It's a very democratic insight," I said. "Not only are all men created equal: all beings, uncreated, are equal. And it's very beautiful."

"But it wouldn't be beautiful if it weren't true."

"On the other hand, there are levels and levels of truth. The deeper you penetrate, the deeper it gets."

"You can appreciate, though," Gabriel said, "how joyful and overjoyful I was. Not to be the highest of created beings, to have no notion any longer of up or down, to be equal to a fly: what freedom!"

"Even though it will be a billion kalpas before you have a chance to enter that place?"

"That didn't matter in the least. It was—is—merely

time. If it will happen eventually, in some sense it is happening now. And in another sense—which I couldn't fathom—since nothing has happened in that state before creation, nothing can ever happen. I was rapt in the recognition. It seemed to me something I had always known. There was nothing more important than that."

"And this was the conclusion?"

"No, there was more. 'In that very being of God where God is above being and above distinctions,' Eckhart wrote, 'I was myself, I wanted myself and understood myself in order to make this man that I am. That is why I am my own cause according to my being, which is eternal, and not according to my becoming, which is temporal. And therefore I am unborn, and according to my unbornness I can never die.'"

"Powerfully stated," I said.

"I felt like kissing him or blessing him or kneeling at his feet. I could barely keep from bursting into song as he wrote the rest of it."

"And you didn't, because . . ."

"I thought it might distract him or somehow get in the way of his momentum. And then, I wanted to save all my attention for his words. 'When I flowed out of God,' he wrote, 'all things said: God exists. But this can't make me blessed, for by this I understand that I am a creature. But when I break through and return where I am empty of my own will and of God's will and of all his works and of God himself, then I am above all creatures and am neither "God" nor creature; but I am what I was and what I will remain now and forever. Then I receive an impulse that will carry me above all the angels. In this impulse I receive such vast wealth that I can't be satisfied with God as he is "God," or with all his divine works; for in this return, what I receive is that I and God are one.'"

"Gorgeous."

"Yes. It's very beautiful. All things return to the One. Thank God."

"Still," I said, "when someone asked old Chao-chou, 'All things return to the One: where does the One return?' he answered, 'When I was in Tsing-chou, I had a robe made that weighed seven pounds.' Now *there* is an example of a mind that's totally free. Ultimate, shmultimate."

Gabriel was silent for a minute or so. Then he said, "I find that impenetrable."

I smiled. "Yes, it's quite something, isn't it? Everyday mind."

"Well, I can't see into it at all. That's the limitation of pure spirit."

"*What* is?"

"Let me ask you this: What did all the heavens you visited have in common?"

"Well, for one thing," I said, "there's no sorrow in them."

"Precisely. And the higher the heaven, the more intense the bliss. In all the angelic heavens there is no trace of past or future sorrow. Our bliss is unmixed with even a particle of its opposite."

"And that's a problem?"

"My dear, we are *attached* to joy. We cling to it, we don't perceive or register any other range of emotion. We don't have the slightest comprehension of sorrow, because—unlike the inhabitants of the human heavens, for whom sorrow is present as the memory of a memory—we have never experienced it. To us it seems as lovely and meaningless as the language of birds."

"I see."

"Every time I visit the earth," he said, "I sense that there is something lacking in our heavens."

"And that something is sorrow."

"Yes."

"You don't feel the lack when you're in your heaven, though."

"No, I am too absorbed in lovemaking or in my games. But at this moment it seems to me that even the most intricate of our games are too easy. There is far too much intelligence and far too little resistance for us to have your kind of challenge. Even our greatest challenges are effortless. The world doesn't push back at us the way it does at you."

"How so?"

"Much of our pleasure comes from creating limitations. Much of yours comes from transcending them. In that sense, we keep heading away from, while you keep heading toward, the *I Am*. It's a good direction."

"I suppose it is. Though it doesn't necessarily make our life any easier."

"Why should it?" he said. "You step out to the very limits of what you can endure. Not a drop overflows, and there isn't room for a single drop more."

"Life does seem like that."

"The fact that your task is exactly as large as your life makes it appear infinite. But your task *isn't* infinite. It's the hidden pretext of a most magnificent game, which in its finiteness includes everything."

"You mean, because it includes both joy and sorrow?"

"Joy and sorrow are the plus and minus of the universe. They are the inhale and exhale of God's breath. In our heavens we know only one pole. We *are* only one pole. The universal current can't pass through us."

"Because the universe is a bipolar system," I said.

"Joy and sorrow are the language of the universe, as zero and one are the language of your computers. We know how to say only 'one.' It's as if we were able to live just inside the major keys. Of course, as it is, there are endless melodies, endless variations, that we can compose ourselves in. But since we don't enter the minor keys, we are playing with only half the tonal resources. *Less* than half."

"And we humans use the minor keys."

"You use everything," he said.

"But what does it mean to be attached to joy?"

"For one thing, we are too happy to grow. There's no reason to. And bliss can go only so far in understanding the *I Am*."

"I'm beginning to get it now," I said. "When there's an excess of happiness, you aren't fully present. You can't be present to the truth that all things arise and disappear, including yourself."

"We have no way of penetrating to where the highest angels and the fly and the soul are equal. The truth of the matter is that without sorrow, there is no growth."

I thought of my decades of inner practice. He was right. After I had with great difficulty learned how to let go, the experiences of intensest suffering, even of horror, were the ones that opened my heart most deeply. Not that I would consciously choose to go through them again, or in the first place. Sitting day after day by the bedside of my child in her unrelievable pain, or witnessing the psychic agony of a beloved friend: these were experiences that I didn't know how I could possibly endure, and yet I endured.

Gabriel looked at me in silence. "I admire that, more than I can tell you," he said. "It is precisely what we are incapable of."

"I think it's the most difficult thing in the world," I said. "To have your heart broken and not contract it or shut it down. To let it break open."

"Well, the human way *is* the way of the broken heart. I would envy you, if envy weren't another mode of sorrow. The fact is—and this is the greatest weakness of an attachment to joy—that because we can't feel sorrow, we can't feel compassion."

"But you know how to *love*. You seem amazingly loving."

"That's true, in certain modes. We accept, we appreciate, we embrace, we feel joy in another's joy. But since we have no capacity for sorrow, we can't enter into it. It's alien to us. We see it uncomprehendingly, the way a human child sees adult sexuality."

"But how is it possible to be loving without being compassionate?"

"You can love only where you enter. And that's why

when angels meet humans, the help we can offer is so limited. Actually, our greatest service is to stand before you as clear mirrors. The compassion that a human may feel coming from us is his own mirrored compassion. The angle of incidence equals the angle of reflection."

"I see."

"It's a considerable lack," he said. "How can we act with the generosity of the great *I Am* if we can't act from compassion? I would sigh, if I could."

"This does seem very much like regret."

"Oh, it will pass in a moment, in the twinkling of an eye, and I won't remember it till the next time I visit the earth, a hundred or a thousand years from now. I will have just completed a game, or disentwined myself from my newest lover, when I'll feel the gravitational pull once again, and find myself suddenly standing before one of you, and suddenly become aware of what is missing. It lasts, in the midst of my delight, for just the briefest of instants."

"You said you don't come here very often, though."

"That I come at all is a testimony to your beauty, lost as I usually am in the inconceivable bliss of our games."

"You're drawn to the beauty of our compassion?"

"To the minus and the plus, the minor key and the major. But especially to the beauty of your compassion."

"So really, it's the bodhisattva that you love in us?"

"That, most of all," he said. "This earth is the realm where bodhisattvas are made. But you humans are very beautiful even when you haven't yet learned to embody compassion. It takes such courage to dive into the ocean

of suffering, unprotected, into the realm where any disaster can happen. For the sake of the soul's growth. In
other words, for the love of God."

"I'm very touched by your admiration."

"But looking at me is, of course, seeing yourself."

"I understand that now," I said.

"And you should remember," he said, "that a mirror
reflects an *image* of who you are. Spirit isn't everything,
you know."

"Thank you. I do know. And I do realize how beautiful we are."

"Then it's time for me to be on my way."

"May I ask you for your blessing?" I said.

"Of course you may, my dear. But there's no need:
you've already found it. Would you like a new name?"

"Thank you, but no. The one I have is just fine."

"All right," he said. "It's been a joy. Maybe I'll see you
again."

"And if I no longer see *you*," I said, "you'll be happy for
me. But this has been wonderful. I love you. Bon voy-
age."

He smiled at me and began to fade. His body became
translucent, then transparent. Then he was gone. I could
hear a faint sound in the inner distance, like the sound of
a door gently closing.

acKnoWLedgmEnts

The paragraph on p. 5 that begins "In me, as the miracle of under-standing" has been adapted and translated from Paul Valéry's prose poem "Un Ange." The quotations on pp. 41 and 42 are from *The I Ching or Book of Changes*, trans. Richard Wilhelm, English trans. Cary F. Baynes, Princeton University Press, 1950. The first quotation on p. 60 is from *The Ten Principal Upanishads*, trans. Shree Purohit Swami and W. B. Yeats, Macmillan, 1937. The koans quoted in chapters II, III, and V have been adapted from Chang Chung-yuan, *Original Teachings of Ch'an Buddhism*, Pantheon Books, 1969. The lines from Yeats quoted on pp. 65 and 230–231 are from "Lapis Lazuli" and "A Prayer for my Daughter," and have been reprinted from *The Collected Works of W. B. Yeats, Volume I: The Poems*, ed. Richard J. Finneran, Macmillan, 1989. The passages from Rilke have been reprinted from *The Selected Poetry of Rainer Maria Rilke*, ed. and trans. Stephen Mitchell, Random House, 1982. The passage on p. 170 that begins "Suddenly a curtain of brilliant white light" and ends "I could see my skin turning gray," and the second and third sentences of chapter VI, have been adapted from *Self-Realization: Life and Teachings of Sri Ramana Maharshi*, by B. V. Narasimha Swami, Sri Ramanasramam, 1976. The dialogue on pp. 182–184 includes passages quoted or adapted from Blake, mostly from "A Vision of the Last Judgment." The paragraph on pp. 191–192 that begins "The next meeting turned out to be a great disappointment" quotes or adapts passages from Buber's foreword to *Pointing the Way: Collected Essays*, trans.

Maurice Friedman, Harper and Brothers, 1957, and from *I and Thou*, trans. Walter Kaufman, Charles Scribner's Sons, 1970. The passage on p. 227 that begins "God's grace is the beginning, the middle, and the end" has been adapted from *Talks with Sri Ramana Maharshi*, ed. M. Venkataramiah, Sri Ramanasramam, 1978. The dialogue on pp. 237–240 includes passages translated from Meister Eckhart's sermon "Beati pauperes spiritu"; they have been reprinted from *The Enlightened Mind*, ed. Stephen Mitchell, HarperCollins, 1990, as have the two sentences, translated from Kafka, on pp. 241–242 that begin "Not a drop overflows" and "The fact that your task."

Yaakov Vitale, Hayim of Verona, Abraham Segrè, Yaakov Yosef of Podolsk, and Benjamin ibn Ezra are imagined characters.

I would like to express my gratitude to Michael Katz, my friend, agent, and sine quo non; to Hugh Van Dusen, my editor, for championing this book at every step along the way; to David Bullen, master designer, for his skill in playing with the Matisse; to Alice Rosengard for reading the manuscript with such bafflement and astuteness; to Vicki Noble for introducing me to Tara; to Joseph Goldstein and Sharon Salzberg for helpful conversations about *metta* practice; to Hillel Levine for the Song of Songs calligraphy; to Thomas Farber, Bob Mitchell, and John Tarrant for their valuable suggestions; to Josh Dunham Wood for taking the dilapidated little two-horse barn on the northwest corner of my property, and designing and building the perfect space for my work, a light-filled studio where these meetings couldn't help but take place.

And to my wife, Vicki Chang, who has met me so deeply and led me into such incarnation: my deepest gratitude of all.